"I was under the ~~impression that~~ you aren't pleased about coming here."

Delfyne's exact words had been that she would rather rot in the royal dungeon than spend a summer on a secluded cattle ranch. "I hadn't fully researched the situation at the time," she said pleasantly. "I hadn't examined the upside of the location. Now I have."

Owen gave a terse nod. He looked down at her hand. "I'm rusty on my royal etiquette. Do I shake your hand, or kiss it?"

His deep voice rumbled, and something primal and earthy and terribly unnerving simmered through Delfyne. She lowered her hand. "I think we'll settle for hello for now." This man, after all, was her jailer, even if he was a reluctant one. She could not and would not feel an attraction to him. He was her brother's friend. He was a commoner. And she was soon to marry.

Still, despite the fact that she should feel nothing for him, she and Owen Michaels were going to be stuck together for a while. She glanced into his flinty, wary eyes. Maybe he had limits, and if she pushed them he'd send her away. She wondered just what Owen Michaels's limits might be.

She would soon find out.

Dear Reader,

My first thought when I decided to write this book was, "How incredibly awesome to be able to marry two of my favorite fantasies in one book!" Because as a child (and way past the time when I could be called a child), I was in love with stories of princes and princesses. There was something about a world so different from my own that enthralled me. It was a world of privilege but also one closed off from so many of the pleasures ordinary people experience.

Then when I grew up and visited the American West, I fell in love with that part of the country. It's big, it's beautiful, it's rugged and still untamed. There are mountains, gorgeous mountains, and there are…ranchers—hardworking, rough, tough guys who never know what hand they'll be dealt from day to day, but who go out there and face their challenges every single day.

So…a princess and a cowboy? Two people whose worlds would ordinarily never intersect? Two people, one tied to the crown and one tied to the land, who could never marry?

What a challenge! What fun! I had to write Delfyne and Owen's story. It begins something (but not exactly) like this:

There once was a princess who was rather disobedient, so her family sent her off to a part of the world where she couldn't get into trouble…or so they thought….

I dedicate this book to those of you who have imaginary princesses inside of them (you know who you are, and yes, if you still like to play dress-up even though you're a grown-up, you *are* a princess at heart), and to those who keep the spirit of the untamed cowboy alive.

And I'm honored to be able to bring you this story in this very special year, when Harlequin celebrates its sixtieth anniversary.

Best wishes and happy reading!

Myrna Mackenzie

MYRNA MACKENZIE

The Cowboy and the Princess

HARLEQUIN®

TORONTO • NEW YORK • LONDON
AMSTERDAM • PARIS • SYDNEY • HAMBURG
STOCKHOLM • ATHENS • TOKYO • MILAN • MADRID
PRAGUE • WARSAW • BUDAPEST • AUCKLAND

Recycling programs
for this product may
not exist in your area.

ISBN-13: 978-0-373-17578-9
ISBN-10:   0-373-17578-7

THE COWBOY AND THE PRINCESS

First North American Publication 2009.

Copyright © 2009 by Myrna Topol.

www.eHarlequin.com

Printed in U.S.A.

Myrna Mackenzie is a self-proclaimed "student of all things that concern women and their relationships." An award-winning author of more than thirty novels, Myrna was born in a small town in Dunklin County, Missouri, grew up just outside Chicago and now divides her time between two lake areas, both very different and both very beautiful. She loves coffee, hiking, cruising the Internet for interesting Web sites and attempting to garden, cook and knit. Readers (and other potential gardeners, cooks, knitters, writers, etc.) can visit Myrna online at www.myrnamackenzie.com, or write to her at P.O. Box 225, La Grange, Illinois 60525, U.S.A.

Don't miss Myrna Mackenzie's
next Harlequin Romance
Hired: Cinderella Chef
August 2009

Western Weddings

In the cowboy's arms...

Imagine a world
where men are strong and true to their word...
and where romance always wins the day!
These rugged ranchers may seem tough on the
exterior—but they are about to meet their match
when they meet strong loving women
to care for them!

If you love our gorgeous cowboys and
Western settings, this miniseries is for you!

Look out for more stories in this miniseries,
only from Harlequin Romance®.

CHAPTER ONE

"OH MAN. There are good ideas and bad ideas, and believe me, sending your sister here so that I can chaperone her is an unbelievably bad idea." Owen Michaels leaned back in his chair and propped his boot-clad feet up on his desk.

"Nonsense, Owen, it's a master plan," the voice on the other end of the line said.

Owen glanced out the window at miles of empty space. Beautiful stuff, if solitude was what you craved. He did. Most people didn't. No denying that. "You been hitting the cognac, Dré? Or…it *has* been a long time since you've been to Montana. Maybe you've forgotten that while I may be a wealthy man, the Second Chance is a working ranch. It's pretty isolated. Your sister's a princess. This isn't what she's used to."

Oh no, Owen thought. *A woman like that is used to a heck of a lot more.* She would crave culture and the excitement of being at the hot, happening center of things. She'd expect to take part in events that involved the cream of society. He already knew too much about women like that. Women didn't transplant well here, as evidenced by his mother, who had run away, and his wife, who had divorced him after—

Owen swore beneath his breath, halting the painful thought. The point was that everything he knew told him that bringing a princess here was a recipe for doom and disaster. "Nope, buddy. What you're asking…it's just not happening. You can't send her here."

"Owen, stop. Let's talk. Or *I'll* talk. You listen. This plan is perfect. Absolutely perfect," Owen's former college roommate said, excitement evident in his voice. "And in answer to your question, I've never been more serious, and no, I haven't been drinking even a little. At least, not since I came up with this solution. Before that, I was going mad trying to figure out what to do with Delfyne."

Andreus's groan brought a frown to Owen's face. "Why do you have to do anything with her?"

His friend sighed. "Because she *is* a princess, one who's getting married soon. As such, she's demanding the summer of freedom from royal life that the rest of us had. It's her right. We all get that opportunity to shake off our bonds once—just once—before we settle in to live our fate."

Owen watched as the almost-too-bright-to-look-at sun began to sink over the landscape, painting the work vehicles red as it began its retreat. When it was finally gone, the darkness would be a black blanket, thick and impenetrable out here where there were no streetlights of any kind, no neighbors for miles. And the silence…well, a person couldn't get much farther from the royal life than this, but Owen was pretty darn sure that that wasn't the kind of vacation Andreus's sister had in mind. "She wants a few months off before she gets married? A trip away from her life? So, what's the problem? Send her on some exotic retreat, or on a cruise or a trip to Manhattan."

"No."

The word seemed a bit too emphatic, and Owen swung his feet off the desk and stood up, dragging the telephone over to the window where he stood in the gathering darkness, watching the clouds turn fiery oranges and purples. "Why?"

Andreus uttered an audible sigh. "Delfyne…is…"

Owen was getting a bad feeling. He turned away from the setting sun and gave all his attention to his friend. "What about Delfyne?" He vaguely remembered meeting Andreus's sister seven years ago when he had been twenty and visiting Andreus in Xenora on spring break. All he remembered was that she had been seventeen, thin and pale, with a posture that had been far more perfect than that of any seventeen-year-old he had ever met. She'd left to visit a cousin in Belgium soon after his arrival. He'd had the feeling that she'd been sent away so that she wouldn't be tainted by the American cowboy running loose in the palace. Even he had to smile at that. Still.

"Delfyne…" Andreus was saying. "My younger sister is… The problem is that Delfyne isn't like our other brothers and sisters. She's lived a sheltered life—a spoiled life in many ways—and she's impetuous and naive. She knows no boundaries and doesn't believe that anything bad can happen to her. She's the girl who had to learn that fire is hot by touching it. Warnings were never enough. Send her out into the world with a total freedom pass and…well, I'm pretty sure you can imagine what could happen."

Silence settled in. Owen could imagine all kinds of things, none of them good.

"Owen?"

"So what you're asking me to do is to babysit your little sister," he said finally.

"Well, I wouldn't put it that way. At least, not to Delfyne's face. She has a temper."

Great. Owen wanted to groan, but, sensitive to the fact that this was his good friend's sister they were talking about, he held back. Just what he needed. A princess with no common sense and a bad temper.

"Andreus…" he tried. "Hell, Dré, you know how unpolished and rough I am. I'm not cut out to take care of a princess."

"Nonsense. Your rough edges will be a boon. You won't let her get into trouble."

"You want me to ride roughshod over a woman?"

Andreus hesitated. "I want you to restrict her a bit."

"Sounds like major babysitting."

"She won't be a problem."

"You just said she was a handful."

"With other people. Not with you."

Owen couldn't hold back a chuckle. "Are you trying to snow me?"

His friend sighed. "Owen, buddy," he said in that stilted way he had. Andreus was a prince through and through. Americanisms didn't come easily to him. "My friend, I'm sure it sounds terrible, but I'm not trying to…to snow you, as you say. You're very good at getting your way and barking orders, aren't you? Remember when I showed up in your dorm room when we were freshmen at the university? I'd been raised a prince, destined to take over the throne. Power was in my blood, but I'd barely made it through the door when you told me which bunk was going to be yours, that you liked quiet when you studied and that you intended to study a lot."

"Yeah, well, I didn't know you were a prince."

"Maybe, but my being a prince didn't seem to matter to you. You treated me like an equal. Like an ordinary person. I appreciated that more than you can ever know. You became my friend. My *best* friend," he stressed.

Owen finally gave in and groaned. "And you saved my butt when four guys jumped me outside a bar. You flew halfway around the world when…"

The pain was still searing even though years had passed. Owen still couldn't say the words. "You helped me when I needed you to," he finished lamely. "I owe you."

"You owe me nothing," Andreus said. "You know I don't operate that way. That's not what this is about. I'm not calling in a favor."

No, that wasn't the kind of man Andreus was. And, Owen remembered, he wasn't the kind of man who asked for favors lightly, either. Despite the lightness of his tone, this couldn't have been easy for him.

"You're really worried about your sister, aren't you?" he asked his friend.

"She holds a special place in my heart, Owen. Delfyne is…sunshine. She's special. And then, too, I know just what she's feeling right now. Being royal has many benefits, but it also provides iron bars that separate a person from the world. Permanently. Freedom to choose one's life is an illusion for a prince or a princess. Her life will never be her own after this time. She knows that."

And what was a man to say to that? Owen valued his freedom and his open spaces above all else. He'd sacrificed other peoples' happiness to that freedom.

And even if his friend would never call his cards in, he owed Andreus his sanity.

"Send her," he said. "Do it. I promise you I won't let anything happen to her and I'll return her to you just as she is now."

"Thank you, Owen. You'll never know what this means to me. You are a saint, my friend."

Owen couldn't help chuckling. "If you think I'm a saint, then you're delusional. But then, I must be delusional, too, saying yes. I hope neither of us ends up regretting this decision."

Of course, it was too late for that, Owen thought as he hung up the phone. Regrets were already pouring in. He'd been called many things in his life. Stubborn, arrogant, rough, a loner. Despite his millions, which would have enabled him to live anywhere he wanted to, he liked his silence and the relative peace he found on the ranch. He'd sacrificed everything for this and he always would.

His peace and his loner status were about to end. A princess was coming to visit the Second Chance Ranch.

"A princess?" Owen muttered when he hung up the phone. "On a ranch? That's crazy talk. Maybe she'll hate it and go back home right away."

A man had to have his hopes and dreams.

Delfyne emerged from her family's private jet, took one look at the very tall man waiting for her and instantly knew that she was in trouble. It wasn't because she found him physically attractive, although she did. What woman wouldn't respond to long legs encased in form-fitting denim, broad shoulders, dark hair and silver-blue eyes? But good looks could be ignored.

What couldn't be ignored was something much more difficult to describe. The expression on his face…this man was a wall, even more of a wall than she remembered from the time he'd visited Andreus years ago. He was a warrior. Stubborn. What's more, he didn't look especially pleased to see her, and she was pretty sure she knew why.

Her brother had told Owen Michaels to look after her. There was no question of that. Because, despite the fact that for her entire life she had been promised this time outside her princess skin, when it came to actually granting her this freedom, every member of her family had been nervous. They'd fussed, they'd tried to give helpful advice without looking as if they were giving helpful advice. Delfyne had come upon her father and Andreus whispering and then acting as if they hadn't been whispering all too often. Because of that and because all her suggestions for places she wanted to stay had been brushed aside with carefully planned criticisms, she'd known months ago that no one was ever going to let her have a true taste of freedom.

They were afraid she was going to make an impetuous mistake…again. Like the time she had slipped away to go swimming alone in the middle of the night and nearly drowned, or the night when one of her maid's daughters had talked her into going to a local town party unescorted and she'd almost been abducted. And yet they didn't know even half the mistakes she'd made as she struggled against the bonds that had always kept her from joy and freedom. She was never going to let them know the very worst thing that had happened to her. She didn't want to think about it herself and she wouldn't, Delfyne thought as the old panic began to rise up.

Still, that didn't mean she was going to spend her life hiding away from the world and from life. She needed this time away from who she was. Just this once to live in the real world, to experience the heady freedom of normalcy, to know what ordinary people knew. She craved that desperately.

But now they had assigned her two bodyguards and a reluctant babysitter and… She glanced at Owen Michaels's square, solid jaw, noting the tension visibly coiled in every muscle in that lean, tough body.

For a moment she felt sorry for him for being stuck watching over her, but she was never going to say that. That would be admitting that he was in charge of her. That wasn't acceptable. She appreciated his hospitality even if it was done as a favor for an old friend, but he was standing between her and her dreams. At least until she could come up with a plan.

Taking a deep breath, Delfyne pasted on the smile she had been trained to wear almost before she had learned to walk and talk. She lifted her head, automatically slipping into regal mode.

"You're Owen, aren't you?" she said, moving toward the man

and holding out one hand in a gracious, queenly gesture. "How very kind and generous of you to offer me lodging during my time here in your United States."

A hint of an amused look lifted the warrior's lips slightly before his grim expression returned. He raised a brow. "You're Delfyne? I was under the impression that you weren't especially pleased about coming here."

Her exact words had been that she would rather rot in the royal dungeon than spend a summer on a secluded cattle ranch. Even though it had been a childish statement to make and even though there was no royal dungeon and never had been. It was simply an expression she and her siblings had used to protest parental rule. It had seldom worked and obviously hadn't worked this time.

Andreus had sung the praises of Montana's wide-open spaces, blue skies, starry nights and the proud, nurturing nature of the people, especially Owen. Her parents had been completely sold on "the Montana plan."

Delfyne had wanted to protest, but a part of her had also been won over, at least a little. She couldn't help being curious about Montana, too, after she'd heard that parts of this place were still wild and untamed. *Like me*, she'd thought.

"I hadn't fully researched the situation at that time," she said pleasantly. "I hadn't examined the upside of the location. Now I have."

"Ah. The upside. You'll have to tell me later what you think that is." The warrior gave a terse nod loaded with meaning, if only she knew what that meaning was. He looked down at her hand. "Meanwhile…I've never actually touched a princess and I'm a bit rusty on my royal etiquette. Do I shake your hand or kiss it?"

His deep voice rumbled, and something primal and earthy and terribly unnerving simmered through Delfyne. She lowered her hand to her side. "I think we'll settle for hello for now. Touching isn't really necessary." This man, after all, was her jailer, even if he was a reluctant one. She could not and would not allow herself to feel an attraction for him. That would be wrong and foolish in so many ways. He was her brother's friend. He was a commoner, and she was soon to marry a man she barely knew but who would bring great connections to her people. She would, of course, do her duty…after she had her taste of life.

Still, despite the fact that she knew she could feel nothing for her brother's friend, she and Owen Michaels were going to be stuck here together for a while unless she could talk him into letting her go off and do all the dazzlingly wonderful and normal things she'd been waiting to do all her life. And unless she could also convince him not to tell anyone about her plans.

She glanced up into his flinty, wary eyes and knew that this wasn't a man who could be convinced easily.

Delfyne withheld a sigh. "Is it very far to your home?" she asked.

He smiled then, and this time his smile looked genuine. And far too dazzling. His silver-blue eyes lit up, and something hot and sparkly zinged right through Delfyne's body, heating up parts of her she preferred to ignore. "Everything is far around here if you're not used to driving distances," her captor-babysitter said. "Are you ready to go?"

She nodded. "Yes." The sooner she assessed her surroundings, the sooner she could figure out how she was going to manage these next few months and what she intended to do either to make this situation palatable or to change it.

Turning toward the airplane, she gave another nod. Immediately, two members of the royal guard appeared. Stoic. Big. Their expressions gave away nothing.

"Who the hell are they?" Owen asked, his voice quiet but

deadly. She thought she heard him say something worse than *hell* beneath his breath.

"My escort," she said simply.

"Your escort," he repeated as if she'd just said she'd traveled here accompanied by flying pink ponies. "They're going home?"

She wished. "If you think you can convince them to leave, you're welcome to try. They follow me everywhere. It's their job."

Owen Michaels frowned. "Any other members of your entourage I should know about?"

For the first time since she'd left home, Delfyne felt like laughing. "I see Andreus didn't tell you about my guards," she said with a smile. "I wonder why."

But they both knew why. Owen didn't want her here, and friendship only went so far. If he'd known he was going to have to house a brooding pair of guardsmen in addition to a princess for months on end, she wondered if he would have agreed to let her stay.

Maybe the man would have said no. Maybe he had limits, and if she pushed them, he'd send her away to where she wanted to go. That was definitely something to think about. Delfyne wondered just what Owen Michaels's limits were.

She would soon find out.

CHAPTER TWO

So ANDREUS'S kid sister wasn't a kid anymore, Owen mused as he led Delfyne to his SUV. She'd been skinny before. Now she was willowy and curvy and stunningly gorgeous, with sable hair and violet eyes. And her legs… He swept his gaze down those sweet legs, ending at a pair of barely there lacy stiletto heels that would have looked at home in a ballroom, a boardroom or…oh yes, they would have looked very fine in a bedroom, but they sure didn't belong on a rough, tough ranch or anywhere near a man like him.

It was all he could do to stop himself from banging his fist on the Land Rover. This was going to be a hellish mistake of an experience. He certainly had no business imagining his calloused palm skimming over a princess's legs.

Frowning, he glanced at her and saw that she was studying him with dismay. And no wonder. He realized that in addition to blatantly eyeing her curves, he had been slamming her bags around and had been silent for several minutes.

"I apologize," he said.

Those pretty violet eyes blinked. "For what?"

Oh, she was good. Her parents had probably trained her to maintain that cool princess aura in the face of bad manners from birth.

Owen shook his head. "I'm supposed to be your host, to make you feel welcome. I don't think I've done that."

She studied him for a moment and then reached out and placed her hand on his arm. Heat shot through his skin and sank deep into his body. Great. Just great. He was lusting after a princess, one who was destined for a prince. What's more, Delfyne was his best friend's little sister, a woman he had sworn to protect, not seduce.

Owen took a deep breath. He forced himself not to look at the point where his skin connected with this beauty's soft palm. She was smiling. No, she was practically dancing, her eyes lit up like twin candles.

"Enough," she said. "Let's not pretend anymore, all right?"

He waited.

She shook her head and, as if she had just realized that she was touching him, looked at her hand and slowly eased it from him. "My brother forced me on you. He and my parents sent me here so that I couldn't be tempted into trouble or so that trouble couldn't be tempted into finding me and hurting me. I'm not your guest, Owen. I'm your short-term obligation. I don't expect you to pretend otherwise."

He considered that. "You didn't want to come to a ranch. This can't be fun for you."

"Well, it's not at all what I'd planned when I planned it."

"When was that?"

She looked to the side and for a second he thought she wasn't going to answer. "I started making my plans when I was eight, when I realized that no matter how carefully I planned my birthday party and no matter how many commoners they reluctantly allowed me to invite, my guests would always be screened, some wouldn't be allowed near me and those that were admitted would be coached on etiquette before they came into my presence. It would never really be a truly free experience completely of my own choosing…except for this one summer."

"I see," he said. And he did. He was another one of those people who was playing the game that kept her from her goals. "Well then, I really am sorry."

She looked at him. "You could let me go my own way."

Owen chuckled. He gestured toward her bodyguards.

"Well, of course I'd take them with me," she said.

And probably ditch them as soon as she was able, Owen thought, remembering what Andreus had told him and trying not to think about the wistful sound in her voice when she'd told him how long she'd been planning her princess prison break.

"Sorry, Princess. I don't lie to my friends, and Andreus is the best. You're mine for a while." Which was such a poor choice of words. "Guest-wise, that is," he added.

"You're not going to do that, are you?"

Okay, she had him there. "Do what?"

"Call me *Princess* as if it's my name."

"It's what you are."

She raised her chin. "Please."

And there was such longing in her voice that he couldn't keep from pursuing the subject. "Please what?"

She hesitated. "I know you've made promises to my family, and Andreus says that you're a very honorable man—the best of men."

Which only showed how deluded and blind Andreus could be, but Owen didn't need to share that information with Delfyne. There was no need to explain his own flawed soul and even more flawed character to her. "I sense a *however* coming on," he said.

The beauty took a deep and visible breath that lifted the pale blue silk of her blouse and made Owen wish that he could do as she asked and send her away.

"All right. You're an honorable man. *However*, I would like to ask one favor of you that would not necessitate you breaking your word to my family," she said in a quiet voice. He could see that, although she was brazening it out, she had no real sense that he was going to do whatever she intended to ask of him. Dread filled him. He had a history of failing women. His mother, his wife and Nancy, who had sought him out last year and *only* wanted him to give her a baby…and now? Damn Andreus.

"Ask," he said, his voice terse. He believed in facing the difficult stuff.

"I… How many people know that I'm here for a visit?"

Owen blinked. "My employees know that I'm having a guest. That's it." He wasn't exactly a sharing kind of man.

"Do they know who I am? What a question. Of course they do, but still…" She seemed distressed.

Frowning, Owen realized what this must be about. Of course. She was royalty, sent to what must seem like Siberia. And yet she would be used to special treatment, the kind she wouldn't think she could get here.

"I'm afraid they don't know you're a princess. At least not yet. I only told them this morning that I would be having a guest. I haven't shared any of the particulars." Because he'd hoped, right up until the last possible moment, that Andreus would realize that this was a bad idea and call the whole thing off.

"But don't worry," he told Delfyne. "I tend to be a bit close-mouthed and that can be a problem at times, but the Second Chance has guests frequently. Usually, they're businesspeople who like the novelty of staying at a ranch, but even with someone more exalted, my employees are up to the task. You'll be treated well."

"That's not my concern. I just… If they don't already know, that's a good thing. I don't want to be a princess."

Owen blinked. He wanted to groan. Surely she wasn't asking him to help her break free of her birthright? "Excuse me?"

A sad look eased into those lovely eyes. "I didn't mean that the way it sounded. Of course I'm proud of who and what I am and glad I'm a member of the royal family. My heritage is important to me. It's just that while I'm here I'd like to remain anonymous," she clarified. "If people know I'm here, there will be newspapers and…"

"And someone might try to harm you or kidnap you," Owen said, looking at the bodyguards, who were standing around trying to fade quietly into a landscape where they stood out like red ink on white paper. He remembered the man who had gone everywhere with Andreus when they had been in college. "I meant what I said when I told Andreus that I'd look after you," Owen said. "No one is going to harm you, and I'm not talking about letting your keepers take care of things. I'm talking about me. *I* wouldn't let anyone get near you."

She shook her head. "But I *want* people near me. That's the point."

Her consternation was clear. However, Owen suddenly noticed Suze Allen driving by and giving him and Delfyne a good looking-over. Suze was a generous creature whom Owen had known for most of his life, but she was like a sieve. Any news that came her way instantly flowed through and out, and a stranger who looked like Delfyne conversing with Owen was definitely going to be news.

"We'd better go," he said suddenly. "Get in the car."

Delfyne looked toward Suze's white pickup, which was circling to come back their way, and to Owen's relief she didn't argue. She let Owen hand her into the Land Rover, and her entourage piled into a black car that arrived from out of nowhere.

"A girlfriend?" she asked when they were on the road to the ranch.

Owen laughed at that. "A gossip, and nothing like a girlfriend, though she's very nice. Suze is married to a man who would punch any man who looked twice at his wife."

Delfyne was silent. For almost five seconds. "Has he ever punched you?" she finally asked.

Owen immediately turned to look at her. "I don't pursue other men's wives, no matter how nice the women are. But that's beside the point. I haven't forgotten what we were talking about before Suze came along. You said that you wanted to be anonymous."

"And you said you wouldn't let *anyone* near me."

He sighed. "Maybe I phrased that badly." He remembered a time when his ex-wife, Faye, had accused him of keeping her trapped in a box. "What I meant was that I wouldn't let anyone or anything hurt you, in case you were worried about that. People from the city sometimes worry about life in a place like this, which is a bit wild. I won't let any harm come to you."

"I never thought you would! Andreus knows you and he trusts you implicitly. That's absolutely good enough for me. I am most certainly *not* challenging your ability to protect me." Now she was indignant…and cute. Somehow he didn't think he should mention that. The word *cute* and royalty probably didn't go hand in hand. "But I meant something more than that. I just— If people know I'm here, there will be reporters, of course, the paparazzi and all that. But that's not my main reason for wanting to stay in the shadows. Ordinary people will treat me differently if they know I'm a princess. I hate that. I *really* hate that."

He could tell. Her voice was terribly sad.

"And I know that's kind of selfish and spoiled," she went on. "I have so much. I've always had so much. I live in a world that most people can't even imagine, but—"

"But you want more," he said. He'd heard that before. Heard his mother telling his father that as she dragged her suitcase out, packed it full of clothes and left him behind, telling Owen to be a good boy before the door closed and she disappeared from his life forever. He'd heard it from Faye as she'd begged him to sell the ranch, take all his money and go somewhere fun and fine. He'd almost decided to do it, too, until his son's death and the total disintegration of his marriage. After that, it had been too late and now he would never leave the Second Chance.

"You're wrong, Owen," Delfyne was saying, and for a moment he thought she'd read his mind. "I don't want more. I want less. Just for this summer, I want to be like everyone else. I want to see what other people see and to live like they do. If people know I'm a princess I can't do that. All right?"

He frowned. Although he could see her point… "I may have kept your visit to myself but now that you're here, this plan sounds like a recipe for disaster. I've never been good at pretense."

"You don't have to pretend. Just leave a few little things out. Like my title."

He couldn't keep from smiling. "Not exactly a little thing."

"Just for this summer. After that—"

They would never see each other again. She would marry her prince, and he would go on with life here at the ranch that had sustained his family for generations. His life would be just the way he liked it. What happened at the end of her time here wouldn't be a problem. But what was happening right now…

"If you're worried about Andreus being upset—" she began.

Now he did laugh. "I promised to keep you free from harm, not to keep from upsetting your brother. He might not have told you this, but I pretty much drove him nuts most of the time we were roommates. I'm stubborn, and so is he. Andreus isn't the problem. I'm just trying to envision the pitfalls if I agree to keep your identity a secret."

A light came into her eyes, and her lips lifted into a smile that made Owen's breath catch. "Think of the pitfalls if you *don't* keep me a secret. You said that your friend—Suze?—was a talker. If she talks and tells a few friends and they tell a few friends and then the newspapers find out, you'll have half the population of Montana lining up outside your ranch."

"You think?" he said, holding back a smile, wondering how far she would take this.

"At least," she said, "Andreus told me that you like your privacy. I'm to behave and not annoy you."

"Are you now?" Owen seriously needed to smile, but he fought the urge.

"I tend to be a bit impetuous at times, and that always annoys my family. Andreus asked me not to do that with you."

"And you don't think pretending you're someone you're not is impetuous?"

Delfyne bit her lip. "Do you?" She twisted her hands in her lap, and suddenly Owen was tired of teasing her. This situation hadn't been created by her or by him. This had been Andreus's idea, and much as he loved the man and owed him, it was a terrible one. Besides, she was right about all of his neighbors and the press coming to call if the truth came out. Heck, he had a ranch to run. He couldn't spend his time dodging reporters. He *did* like his privacy.

No, he *needed* his privacy. If the press came calling, they would want to know about Delfyne but also about the man keeping her here. Then they would want a little history, and if they delved into his background, the tragedy of his past… He didn't want anyone writing sob stories about how he'd lost his child and his wife and now a beautiful, unattainable princess had come to call.

Owen's blood chilled at the thought.

"Who do you want to be?" he demanded suddenly.

She stared straight into his eyes. "Just Delfyne. That's all. Just an ordinary woman."

Oh yeah, people were going to believe that this woman was

ordinary. She had a foreign lilt to her voice, skin like expensive silk and a body that would make even the tamest of men take notice. But he hadn't been lying when he'd said that he wasn't good at pretending. He'd leave that part to her.

"Here we are," he said as he made the last turn and the house came into view.

"Oh my."

Yes, that just about said it all, didn't it? "Not exactly what a princess is used to."

"It's built of logs!"

"You noticed that, did you?"

"But…it's also very big."

That was being kind. The house meandered and had a huge wraparound porch. It filled up a lot of space.

"I have a habit of building when I need to think. Or not think."

"You must need to think—or not think—a lot. Andreus never mentioned this."

"Yes, well, I guess the subject of architecture doesn't come up a lot in royal conversations." But it was more than that, Owen knew. Andreus knew of the depth of the private pain that had triggered Owen's building craze. He wouldn't have spoken of Owen's feelings to anyone without asking his friend's permission first.

"And this is all for one person? I mean…that is…"

Owen held up one hand. "You know I'm divorced and that I lost my son. I have a housekeeper and cook, Lydia Jeffers, who comes by, but I'm the only one who lives here. The hands live in the bunkhouse. And yes, it's a lot of house for one person. I justify the space by having a few gatherings here each year. The local cattlemen's association holds their annual conference here and if my neighbors need overflow housing for their guests, I've been known to oblige them. Which means you probably make a good point about staying here incognito. I have a feeling that if your status becomes known, I'll be overrun with unexpected guests."

He parked in front and blew out a breath, then climbed from the Land Rover and circled around to assist Delfyne from the vehicle.

She beat him to it. "All right. If I get to be who I want to be, then I'm an independent woman for the next few months. No special considerations. I'll open my own car doors and do...oh, whatever I like. All the things princesses aren't allowed to do."

The excited smile she gave Owen caught him by surprise, full-force. Damn, but what had Andreus been thinking sending his sister here to stay with a bad-tempered recluse like himself? The woman clearly belonged in the sunshine. Her smile practically sparkled. She all but danced up the porch stairs, then turned, tipped her face up to him and held out her hands. "Thank you so much, Owen. You don't know what this means to me. I'm going to be an anonymous, blend-into-life woman!"

Blend in? Owen didn't think so. On this ranch she was going to stand out like a rose among thistles, and the way she was looking at him as if he'd just offered her the keys to a long-sought treasure...

Don't even think about her that way, Owen told himself. He'd learned he didn't have much other than money to offer most women, so getting entangled with a woman with a crown would be an act of major stupidity. No, the best thing he could do was to get Delfyne set up as he had promised her brother and then put a lot of space between himself and her.

"I'll get your things inside and show you where your room is," he said. "Your bodyguards can stay in the bunkhouse. I'll tell my employees that they're friends of yours who want to experience ranch life. It won't be the first time I've had that type of guest."

"All right. Owen?"

He looked up. She was staring at him in that direct, unnerving way she had. "What?"

"I know I said thank you already, but I want you to know that it wasn't just a cursory expression of gratitude. I really do know how much my family owes you for allowing me to stay here. Beyond the difficulties of hiding a princess in your house, Andreus told me that you don't like women much."

Her voice was soft, the expression in her eyes even softer. Something low in Owen's gut shifted. His body went on full alert, and he felt a growl coming on. His conviction earlier that having this woman at his house was a bad idea deepened. Because Andreus was dead wrong. It wasn't that he didn't like women. He just couldn't offer what most of them wanted, so it was better to keep his distance most of the time.

With this woman he could tell that it would be better to keep his distance *all* of the time. Too bad that was going to be impossible.

"So…thank you very much for giving me a place to stay," Delfyne finished. "That was very kind of you."

Oh yeah, he was going to start letting her think that he was kind. That wasn't going to happen. If he did, she'd turn those mesmerizing violet eyes on him and then…he wasn't going to think about what he might do then. Something idiotic and wrong. He had his limits.

"So Andreus told you that, did he? That I was being kind?"

She slowly shook her head. "No, he told me that you thought you owed him something because he came over here when…when you needed a friend. You're doing this out of a sense of obligation."

Which *was* the truth, so he said nothing.

"But agreeing to pretend I'm someone other than who I am…that took guts. Andreus and my family won't like that at all. They think that pretending to be an ordinary citizen will leave me vulnerable." For a second she looked a bit uneasy. "My family thinks that if men don't realize who I am or what my destiny is, they'll try to take liberties."

Great. Now Andreus was going to want to kick his butt, and the man would be right. Owen hadn't actually thought of this particular problem.

"Don't worry. I won't let anyone near you," he reiterated. *Including me.*

Which didn't exactly bring a smile to her face.

"I told you I don't want to be a prisoner here."

He scrubbed a hand over his jaw. "Let me amend my last statement. I won't let the wrong kind of people near you. You can have total privacy."

Still, no smile.

"Delfyne, I'm doing my best. Princesses aren't exactly my area of expertise."

She nodded. "Okay, that's fair. What is your area of expertise?"

"Ranching and making money. That's pretty much it."

"And building," she reminded him.

"Yeah, well, that's not an expertise. That's an obsession."

She did smile then. "Ah, obsessions. I understand those. I have a few of my own." But she didn't elaborate.

And there they stood, the princess and the rancher. Owen looked at the beautiful, cultured woman who had dropped into his world. He wondered how he was going to survive this experience. He glanced out into the distance, to his land. To his cattle. To the roots and the history that kept him mostly sane.

"I'm sorry. You have work to do. Andreus warned me not to be a pest. If you show me to my room, I'll get settled in. And, Owen, don't worry. I know you didn't exactly want me here and I didn't want to be here, but you've given me the gift of a chance to be myself and I intend to take it. Don't worry about the privacy. I don't need it. Now that I know we're agreed that I can take a vacation from being a princess, I can't wait to let loose and be who I want to be and do what I want to do. I won't be a bother at all. You'll barely notice that I'm around."

Owen wanted to throw back his head and howl at that. Oh yes, he had made a big mistake saying yes to Andreus, Owen thought as he showed the two guards to the bunkhouse then strode toward the ATV that would take him out to where the rest of his hands were mending fence.

This woman was unpredictable. She wanted things she couldn't have, and Owen had far too much experience with women who wanted things they couldn't have. It always turned out badly.

He was going to spend as little time as possible with the princess who was inhabiting his house. A man would be insane to do anything else.

CHAPTER THREE

DELFYNE had gone online and ordered some "ordinary-woman" clothes, but two days hadn't been enough time for them to arrive, so this morning she opted for the least glamorous things she owned. The pale blue slacks and white silk blouse weren't exactly casual, but they would have to do.

She delved into her jewelry box and came up with what she wanted. "Finally! A chance to wear these!" She placed the yellow, blue and white bangle bracelets on one wrist and the cute bracelet with the gaudy pink elephant charms on the other.

Then she slipped bone-colored ballet flats on her feet and ventured out into the house, wandering the massive hallways. This was very much a man's house. Everything was big and spare with clean lines and no frills. Golden wood was everywhere.

There was art on the walls. Expensive art, she noted, but no personal items. No photographs, no mementos of any type. And most of the rooms looked as if they were seldom used, which was probably the truth. Altogether there was little here to tell her about her host, about the man.

She knew some things, of course, the little that Andreus had told her in the past or had felt she needed to know now. Owen had once had a wife, a gorgeous blonde he'd met in college. They'd married and he'd taken her back to the family spread.

Eventually, they'd had a son who had died of Sudden Infant Death Syndrome. Then the marriage had dissolved. That was all Delfyne knew other than the fact that Owen was very rich. He'd spent his alone time doing more than just building this house. He'd invested his money in a mix of risky ventures and conservative stocks and had earned a fortune. But he seldom left the ranch. Andreus had tried to get him to visit their palace on Xenora several times to no avail, other than that one trip when the two of them had been in college. So Owen was a man of mystery.

And now he was *her* man of mystery, temporarily.

Delfyne's breath caught at the expression. She knew better than to have those kinds of thoughts. Much as she wanted to have some adventures, she didn't want to have romantic ones. Already she'd learned that being a princess—an impetuous princess—had its downside. Men had taken advantage of her and misread her enthusiasm for life as something more. The fact that she was destined eventually to marry a royal and couldn't ask for a commitment had encouraged the few men she'd known to try and take advantage of her. So no, no man of mystery for her. No men at all in a romantic sense.

The fact that Owen was rugged and good-looking with fierce, compelling eyes had to be immaterial. He was her host, no more, and he was a reluctant host at that. He didn't like having her foisted on him.

That was probably why, during the two days she'd been here, she'd barely seen him at all. When she got up in the morning, he was gone. Apparently he ate his meals elsewhere, and she had no idea when he came in or what he did all day.

What she did know was that her glorious plans for independence were fading away. She'd spent the two days alone or bugging Lydia Jeffers just so she would have someone to talk to.

Lydia, while she was a very nice woman, had work to do and she seemed suspicious of who and what Delfyne was.

None of this was getting Delfyne what she wanted—a taste of real life.

Something had to happen soon. Something good and exciting and different. The hourglass held only so much sand and once she returned to Xenora, her life would never be her own again. Not a minute of her time here could be wasted.

"So, that's it, then. Owen may not like having me here, but I won't be locked away in the house reading books and eating bon bons. The man is just going to have to put up with me," she declared to the empty walls. Pushing open the door, she wandered out into the green and misty morning.

Immediately, her bodyguards, Theron and Nicholas, stood up from where they'd been sitting. She waved them away. Yesterday she'd explained to them their role as greenhorns trying a taste of ranch life, but they didn't seem to be getting into the spirit of things.

"Go. Do something," she said.

"What?"

"I don't know. Eat."

Theron laughed. He sat down again. She ignored him and continued on her way.

The scent of growing things and something animal filled her nostrils and she breathed in deeply, acclimating herself to the unfamiliar. This was the perfume of life, not the palace.

Staring around her, Delfyne took in the endless miles of land, the buildings that were clearly not living space and a number of big, hulking, unfamiliar vehicles.

She smiled as Jake and Alf, two of the ranch dogs, ran around barking as if vying for her attention, jumping around so much that Alf nearly stepped on the paw of a little orange cat that came too close.

"You two behave yourselves," she ordered affectionately, scratching Jake behind the ears. "And watch where you're walking. You nearly squashed this little guy."

Indeed, the cat was limping slightly, but when Delfyne tried to pick him up he gave her a look that said, "I'm a rough tough ranch cat. I don't need coddling," and continued on his way.

She knew the cats here had no names. They were working animals, not pets, and there were too many of them. "But I'm calling you Tim," Delfyne announced to the cat's retreating back. "As in Tiny Tim."

Her parents would have groaned. Her father in particular had worried about her tendency to request bedtime stories with happily-every-after endings. He'd taken to giving her warnings about the tales, telling her that in the original story of *The Little Mermaid*, the heroine had not married her prince, and that in her favorite Xenoran legend, King Vondiver, the hero, had given up his crown to pursue his love of a common woman and had suffered a terribly alarming, sad and lonely ending. Surely she didn't want to end up like that.

Her parents needn't have worried. Delfyne knew that stories weren't real, and she had absolutely no desire to have her life turn out like the endings of those tales. She just liked hearing them. Vondiver's story in particular always left her misty-eyed.

"Getting teary over a silly story can be downright embarrassing, Tim," she said.

The cat continued to ignore her, and Jake and Alf had already run off, attracted by something else.

"On my own again," Delfyne said with a sigh. "But I refuse to feel sorry for myself. Princesses don't. When we find ourselves in less-than-ideal circumstances, we do something about it!

"So stand tall," she said, quoting from that ever-present supply of lessons that had been fed to her as a child.

Some princesses might take that a step further and take action, she thought. Okay, that had never been part of her lessons. It was from her own personal, flawed guidebook…which meant she was on the verge of doing something ill-advised. "But I have to do *something*," she muttered.

She looked around again. Owen was nowhere to be seen, so Delfyne continued on toward one of the large structures. Was it the barn, perhaps? She had no idea, but she wasn't about to be deterred now that she'd made up her mind to escape the house. She was almost to the door when she heard a rustle and a shout.

"Damn it, Ennis, stop messing around and get over here and help me!"

That was unmistakably Owen's voice. It was coming from the structure next to this one. Delfyne didn't hesitate. She followed Owen's voice, slipping inside the building.

What she saw stopped her in her tracks.

There was Owen, all broad shoulders and lean hips, his damp shirt plastered to his body as he bent over a cow that had its head in some sort of contraption. He shook his head toward the man standing beside him. Ennis, Delfyne assumed.

"Get Len. We're going to have to operate," Owen said. "This calf isn't coming, even with the chains. And when you get back, wash up. Make sure this area is disinfected. Come on. Hustle. She's suffering."

His words brought Delfyne's attention back to the cow, which did appear to be in serious distress. And that contraption…

A small sound escaped Delfyne, and Owen looked up. A curse word escaped him.

"Go back to the house," he told her.

His tone brooked no opposition. She bit her lip.

"What are you going to do to her? That machine doesn't look comfortable."

Was that a growl? "It's not, but it's necessary so she doesn't hurt herself or kick out and kill one of us while we help her. Now go. You don't belong here."

"Will she be all right?"

He grimaced and started to answer. She was pretty sure he wasn't going to offer her any platitudes, but she'd never know that for sure because a man shrugging into a pair of pristine coveralls came loping in at that moment and started barking orders. He must be the vet.

"Ready, boss?" the man asked.

"She's yours, Len," Owen answered, but he didn't move away. Instead, he deftly assisted the man, following Len's orders quickly and efficiently, as if he'd done this hundreds of times before.

"She's bleeding too much," Len said. "Give me the hemostat. Come on. Quick. Quick, dammit."

Owen slapped the object in the man's hand and Len went to work. There was so much blood.

Delfyne felt light-headed and weak. She reached for the wall and tried to stay quiet. Apparently unsuccessfully, because Owen swore and started toward her. "You look like you're going to faint. I'm getting you out of here now."

But when he moved toward her and away from the cow, Delfyne realized that the animal might not survive because "the princess" had drawn Owen's attention and hands away from the task at hand.

"No. No, I'm all right. Go help." She motioned him back, gulping in air. Her voice was shaky but she remained standing.

He hesitated.

"Owen!" Len was yelling.

"Go!" Delfyne yelled, too. She had a crazy urge to say, "I command you," even though she'd never said that in her life.

Without another word, Owen returned to his place with Len

and the distressed creature. Side by side, the two men barked orders at each other and worked in concert, a team that had obviously done this together before.

They made another incision and eased out the calf. Owen checked it over and gently laid it aside. Then he turned back to its mother. Based on the men's brief, guttural exchanges, Delfyne caught the merest hint of what was happening. Antibiotics were involved. She heard the word *antiseptic*. Stitches were made. Finally, Ennis took the apparently healthy calf away and then came back for the woozy, tipsy but on-her-feet mother, promising to keep watch over both of them. He glanced at Delfyne, a question in his eyes, but he said nothing.

Len was obviously less cautious about asking questions. After washing up and changing his coveralls for a clean shirt, he came over and held out his hand, flashing her a devilish smile that she was sure he reserved for women he was interested in. "Well, hello there, pretty mystery lady. You must be one of the visitors we were told about. I'm Len Mayall. And you're…"

"None of your business, Len." Owen's words were quiet but firm as he came up behind them. He had shed his shirt and put on a new one but he hadn't had time to button it yet. Delfyne tried not to notice what a fine, muscular chest he had, but her fingertips tingled. And he had said—

Delfyne frowned sternly and gave Owen a pained look. "I'm Delfyne," she said.

Which clearly wasn't what Len had wanted to know, by the questioning look he gave Owen. Now she got it. He wanted to know what her relationship to his boss was.

"Yes, I'm a visitor," she said with a smile. "I'll be staying for quite a while."

Len's eyebrows rose. "I see."

Owen moved closer to the man who had been wielding a

scalpel moments before. He had deferred to Len then, but now he towered over him. There was no question who was the boss.

"No, you don't see. Delfyne is—"

Uh-oh, Owen was going to say "a princess," wasn't he? Or something of that nature. Because he wanted to make it clear to Len that he was not romantically linked to Delfyne.

Delfyne couldn't let him say that. "Owen was kind enough to take me in when I needed a place to stay," she said, rushing in. Which still didn't seem to do the trick. Len's eyes opened even wider.

He looked at Delfyne's expensive clothes. "Pardon me, Delfyne, but if you're from around these parts, I'll swallow my scalpel. You're just too darn beautiful for me to have forgotten you. So where in the universe did Owen find you? And are there any more like you? You say he…*took you in?*" His tone was incredulous.

Delfyne blinked. Yes, she supposed that did make it sound as if she'd been plucked from the streets. Owen's brows drew together in a scowl.

"Len," he said, his voice low and gravelly and cool. "You're a fine veterinary student and a good hand, and you know that I would be hard-pressed without you, but right now you're skating on ice so thin I can hear it cracking beneath your feet. Delfyne is a *friend*, a new one, and I'd prefer that you not act as if your mother never taught you any manners by asking her a lot of nosy questions." Owen paused, his hands on his hips, his scowl deepening. "The truth is that Delfyne wanted to see some of the world, and she's never been to Montana. She and her friends Theron and Nicholas will be visiting for a few months. As to where their home is, that's none of your business. I don't like having my guests interrogated. I also don't like them to be talked about…by anyone. I hope I'm clear on that."

Len held up his hands in a gesture of surrender. "Got it, Owen.

You're right. I was out of line, ma'am," he said, backing away but not looking all that sorry. "I'll just get my sorry rear out of here before I get fired. Morgan and a couple of the boys will disinfect everything here, boss," he said. "You see to your guest."

But as she and Owen walked away, she could swear she heard something very low that sounded like "A few months?"

She glanced back over her shoulder and saw that Len was grinning. "By the way, nice meeting you, Delfyne. Your secret, whatever it is, is safe with me, but I have to tell you, you're the prettiest guest this ranch has had in…oh, just about forever."

When she turned back around, Owen was striding away, his white shirttail flapping around his hips. She ran to catch up with him. When she drew even with him, she could see that his mouth was drawn into a thin line. His jaw looked granite-hard.

"I came in at a bad time, didn't I?" she asked. "And I embarrassed you with your friend."

He turned that ice-blue stare on her. "Len is a pain in the— he's a pain, sometimes. But he's a good vet, or he will be when he finishes his training. He knows he'd have to do something pretty heinous for me to fire him, and he likes mouthing off. He especially likes women," he pointed out.

"I could tell."

Owen chuckled. "I'm sure you could. I'd like to see Len's eyes roll back in his head if he found out he was trying to flirt with a princess. That would shut him up."

"Don't be so sure. Sometimes knowing a woman is forbidden brings out the worst in men."

Owen studied her carefully. "I don't intend for you to see the worst side of any man around here. I owe Andreus a great deal. Letting his little sister be harassed isn't in the cards while you're here. I'll keep Len away."

She frowned. "You don't have to. Len seems harmless."

Owen's frown intensified. "If he thinks he can get you into bed, he'll use all the charm he has to do it. Women tend to fall for Len. Sometimes I think that's why he's taking so long to finish his training. Not being licensed yet leaves him with more time for his love life. None of those middle-of-the-night calls that full-fledged veterinarians get."

"You think I'd be susceptible to someone so obvious?"

"I think I don't know you at all, so I can't answer that. I do know that friend or not, Len's just the kind of man Andreus would want me to protect you from."

She raised her chin.

To her consternation he smiled.

"What?" she asked.

"Your identity may be a secret, but your manner is purely royal."

"I'll have to work on that, then. My manner…these clothes… Len knew I didn't fit in, and I don't. I want to become part of the woodwork, to be a part of my surroundings."

"Sort of an experiment," he suggested.

"No. A life experience. I want to immerse myself."

"Well, you certainly got a good start with what happened back there with that cow and her calf."

"It was…interesting."

He laughed out loud then. "Did they teach you diplomacy before you learned how to walk? You nearly fainted. And…I understand your desire to have some fun and live a little before you get on with your life, but Andreus must have taken leave of his senses. This is no place for someone like you."

And even though he was right in some ways—this ranch was not the place she would have chosen to spend this summer— Delfyne couldn't help but bristle a bit.

"I didn't faint. I'm not just fluff."

"I didn't say that."

"You implied it." She couldn't keep the slight edge and the hint of hurt from her tone, and to her surprise he reached out and gently grasped her chin.

"I guess I did, and I'm sorry about that. Len would tell you that I'm more of a pain than he is, and I guess I'm the one who should be told off for having bad manners instead of him, because no, you didn't faint."

His hand was warm against her skin, his touch was doing terrible, wonderful things to her senses. As if he suddenly realized his effect on her, he released her. "Timing is important when life hangs in the balance. The fact that you sent me back to work enabled us to get the job done, for which I'm grateful, but that doesn't change things. It doesn't mean that I think this is a good place for you. And yes, I can be silent about who you are, but I can't ignore it.

"This is a ranch, Delfyne. It's a big ranch and a prosperous one, but even the biggest ranches revolve around cattle. Animals. Heavy, dangerous machinery. There's a lot of dirty work, some blood, a ton of sweat and a fair amount of muck. Most of my men are regulars, but sometimes for the short term there are rough, transient workers about, and there are plenty of things a woman like you wouldn't ordinarily be exposed to. I can't like that. What *were* you doing out there, anyway?"

She hesitated. Her first instinct was to say that she had spent two days alone and wanted company. But that sounded a whole lot like, "I'm bored," the whining of a pampered princess.

"I need to do something," she said instead.

"In the calving shed?" Was he smiling? Was he laughing at her? Somehow the thought didn't offend her. It cheered her up.

She laughed. "Oh, is that what you call that place? I had no idea. Will the cow and her baby be all right?"

She expected him to say yes automatically, the way people

did. "Probably," he said instead. "Len is careful but there's always the danger of infection. One of the men will check in on the two of them round the clock tonight."

It occurred to her that in his line of work he probably saw a lot of sickness and more. "Did you ever…I don't know…keep one of them? Name it?"

He stopped and faced her, his shirt still hanging open, his bare chest gleaming in the sun. For a second she felt faint again and she fought not to sway. "This is a ranch, Delfyne. It's not smart to get attached. *I* don't get attached. I know the rules and I always live by them."

She was pretty sure that he was talking about more than cows. She also knew that he was being smarter than she was, but she was going to be here for several months. This situation—living alone with nothing to do—was unacceptable.

"I need to do more than lounge around reading," she said. "You may think that's what—" she glanced to the side "—princesses do," she whispered. "But I'm not that useless."

"All right." He placed his hands on those lean hips. "What kinds of things are you used to doing?"

She thought about that, about the charities and the school and library openings, the things she was good at and would continue to be good at for the rest of her life. But…

Delfyne shook her head. She didn't want to tell him what she did, because she was sure that he would consider it to be inconsequential. The hilarity of that—that a princess should be concerned that a commoner might not think well of her—didn't escape her, but it didn't change the truth, either.

She wanted Owen Michaels to respect her. She hated the fact that he considered her a bit of a pest, an obligation, his friend's annoying little sister who had been foisted on him. She knew now that he would never send her elsewhere. His sense of duty to her brother was too great. But neither would he be happy until he had carried out his duty and sent her back to her family. He wanted her gone…preferably yesterday.

Anger rose up within her. Wanting a man to like her had gotten her into major unforgettable, never-get-past-it trouble before. She wouldn't play that role again, and she wouldn't ever allow a man to make her cower and cringe and beg again.

So, she stepped closer to him. She dared to do what she wouldn't have done a few minutes earlier. She placed her hand on his bare chest.

It had been meant to be an imperious gesture, a way of showing that she was beyond being affected by him and a way of emphasizing what she was about to say. Instead, instant heat pulsed through her body and it was all she could do to keep herself from leaning toward him. She could feel his heartbeat beneath her fingertips, strong and solid and powerful. There was something very masculine about it, and something much too personal about what she was doing. But if she pulled away too quickly, he would know that he had unnerved her.

"I just want you to know that I'm *not* going to play the part of the prima donna, lounging around drinking champagne, eating chocolates and giving air kisses to everyone." She fought to keep the angry edge to her words, to hold on to what she hoped would pass as imperiousness that could not be denied.

"Air kisses?" His hand covered hers, and now her own heart was thundering.

"You know," she said, losing the battle, her voice coming out soft and strangled. "Where you bring your face close and pretend to kiss someone but you really don't?"

Now he smiled. "I know what an air kiss is. I just… Do you really think that I believe you do all those things? You don't, do you?"

Slowly, she shook her head. "Hardly ever."

"So you're going to continue *not* to do those things you don't do, anyway. Delfyne, I have absolutely no experience with princesses, so tell me…what *are* you going to do? What do you *want* to do?"

"Everything," she said. And for some reason she couldn't explain, she looked at his lips. Longing washed over her, and she knew darn well that it was completely wrong. The one thing she knew she *wasn't* going to do was develop a crush on Owen Michaels. Or on any man, for that matter. But especially not this one. He would hurt her. She knew that…so clearly.

It was that thought and only that thought that enabled her to step back and away from him.

"Just so you know," she told him. "I want to do everything."

For several seconds he said nothing, but his eyes said it all. He was not a happy man.

"Define *everything*," he finally said.

But she had had enough. Besides, she didn't have a clue about the specifics of what she had meant.

"I'll make it up as I go along," she said.

"Don't make me regret saying yes to Andreus's request," he said.

Which was the perfect thing to break the tension. Delfyne laughed and headed for the house. "Too late. I know that you've regretted it from the start, haven't you?"

He didn't answer, and for some reason that fact was still bothering her hours later.

CHAPTER FOUR

ALL RIGHT, Owen thought the next day while he was freeing a cow that had gotten stuck in a broken bit of fence. Delfyne had been here only a few days and already she was playing havoc with his world and also—he didn't even want to think about this—his senses.

It had been a mistake to touch her. Her skin had been soft, softer than any woman's skin he could remember. And her lips had been so close that he'd wanted to swoop in and taste. He'd wanted his hands on more than just her chin.

"Get a grip, Michaels," he ordered himself. He was fantasizing about kissing a princess, one who was going to marry a prince. Besides the fact that finding himself with some sort of fatal attraction was really on his list of things never to do, a man would have to be some sort of idiot to put his hands on a forbidden woman.

"That frown on your face can't mean anything good. Do you need help with that cow?"

Owen looked around to see Ennis approaching in an old open-top Jeep. The man stared at the cow, who was bawling loudly but standing still.

Owen was glad that he wasn't a man to redden up with embarrassment. "No, my mind was just wandering," he admitted as he freed the patient animal. "I do need you to mend this fence, though."

"Done."

"I thought you were changing the oil in the truck."

"I was. Lydia sent me to get you."

"Lydia?" She'd worked for him for years and had never sent for him unless there was an emergency. "What's wrong?"

"I don't know, but I gather it has something to do with your gorgeous, exotic visitor."

Owen's head swiveled around and he looked at Ennis, who had worked for him for five years and been the most circumspect of men. "Gorgeous, exotic visitor?"

Ennis held up his hands. "I'm just saying…"

"Yeah, well, you better not let Alice hear you 'just saying…'"

Grinning, Ennis went to the Jeep and got his tools. "Alice was the one who told me Delfyne was gorgeous and exotic."

"Really? What else did your wife say?"

Ennis gave him a look. "She said that if any woman could jolt you out of your 'idiotic ways with women' Delfyne could."

Owen scowled. "What idiotic ways?"

"Oh, I don't know," Ennis mused, squatting to get closer to the fence. "Maybe the ones where you bed them but never wed them."

"Is that right? Well, Ennis, you know how much I adore your wife, but she's dead wrong on this one. Delfyne is getting married when she goes home."

"Hmm, Alice isn't going to like that. She was hoping for the chance to go to a wedding. *Your* wedding."

Owen smiled. "Send her my condolences, but it's not happening. She'll have to find some other wedding to attend. You're sure you don't know what Lydia wants?"

"She just said that she had some important questions to ask you. And she said that you needed to give her a raise if she was going to have to worry about Delfyne hurting herself or setting the house on fire. Maybe you'd better hurry."

Ennis chuckled as Owen swore, hopped on his ATV and started to take off.

"Oh, Alice says she wants you to come to dinner on Saturday, and she wants you to bring Delfyne, too."

"Tell her thank you, but I don't think I'll be able to make it."

"She'll be disappointed."

Owen stopped and looked at Ennis, his employee and friend. "I'm sorry."

He was, too, he thought as he sped away on the ATV. Alice was a sweetheart and she was good for Ennis. She was good to everyone, and she tried to fix people's troubles, including his. She'd started inviting him to dinner not long after Faye had gone, but…Ennis and Alice had two kids, sweet little munchkins. The very sight of them seared his soul and hurt his heart. How could you tell a man and his wife that the children that gave light to their lives ripped your world apart even as you thanked God for putting them on the earth? He begged off on dinner as much as he could, especially since Alice tended to invite women she thought might fill what she perceived as a hole in Owen's life. Now, if he went with Delfyne, after what Ennis had said…

"I'm really sorry, Alice, hon," he said out loud to the wind. "It isn't happening." What *was* happening, he saw as he hopped from the vehicle and strode into the house, was that something had exploded in his kitchen.

"Come on. Let me do that," Lydia was saying.

"No. I messed everything up and I will fix it." Delfyne's lilting accent floated out, its sexy timbre sending his body into full alert. *Don't react*, he ordered himself. *Don't feel. Don't desire.*

Instead he moved further into the mess, catching both Lydia's and Delfyne's attention. They both looked up, and Owen saw that Lydia, while clean, was flustered and concerned. Delfyne's face was radiant…and covered in numerous smudges of white. Her dark satiny hair had traces of white here and there, too. The kitchen was coated in what appeared to be flour.

"Problem?" he asked as innocently as he could.

"I'm trying to cook," Delfyne declared, "but I hadn't quite realized just how heavy a twenty-pound bag of flour could be."

"Hmm, I see. Cook a lot, do you?" Okay, she looked so proud of herself that it was difficult to keep the amusement from his voice. His state-of-the-art kitchen had never looked so distressed and neither had Lydia, at least not in his memory.

"This is my very first time," Delfyne admitted. "I've practically given Lydia a heart attack. Lydia, don't be upset. I will take care of the mess."

Lydia was shaking her head. "That's not why I'm upset. A little mess isn't going to kill me. You just stop right there. Put that broom down. I mean it, darn it. I'm the one who's cleaning this up. Don't make me wrestle that broom away from you."

Lydia's voice brooked no argument. She was a decent-sized woman and a stern one. Stronger men than he had fled when Lydia gave an order. But Delfyne just wrinkled her nose and grinned. "Lydia, I'm sorry but I cannot allow you to do that."

Uh-oh, the queen of the kitchen and the princess from birth were about to have some issues over who was in charge. But Owen knew Lydia well enough to know that what was bothering her went deeper than maintaining control of her domain.

"Excuse us, Delfyne," he said, motioning to Lydia, who followed him out onto the patio. "Okay, spill it. What's happening and why are you so upset?"

"Owen, that girl is a guest here. And my lands, she's clearly never set foot in a kitchen before, at least not to make a meal. This morning she tried to light that old gas stove that we only use when we have extra-big affairs, and she nearly blew her head off. I swear my heart stopped dead for five whole seconds. What are you about, having your house guest messing in the kitchen when she should be seeing the sights?"

Good question. He knew the answer—he didn't want to take her out to "see the sights," such as they were, for fear that sooner or later someone would figure out who Delfyne was and the world would come running. They would spoil her vacation from royalty and they'd post his son's photo all over the newspapers and the Web. Heartbroken Rancher Heals his Sorrow over Loss of his Child by Falling for Princess, or something obscene like that. But he couldn't tell Lydia that, at least not all of it. To Lydia, Delfyne had to be just another guest.

"She values her privacy and isn't really into sightseeing. And, Lydia, look at her," he said, motioning to Delfyne, who could be seen through the window. "Does she look unhappy?"

Lydia grunted. "She looks way too happy for a woman who is sweeping the floor."

He laughed. "Lydia, I know you're not used to sharing your kitchen, but I'm asking you…share it, teach her what she wants to know. Ennis mentioned you wanted a raise, so yes, there's a raise in it for you."

Lydia blushed. "You know I didn't mean that when I said it. I was talking off the top of my head because I was upset."

"Nonetheless, you're getting one. I've been paying you to cook, not give cooking lessons, so now that I'm asking you to do that, too, I'll pay you more."

Lydia gave him a grateful smile and a thank-you. "I'd better go help her clean up. If we're going to start lessons, we'll need a clean kitchen."

"All right, but let me talk to her first. Give me fifteen minutes."

She nodded. "I'll just do a little weeding in the kitchen garden."

Owen stepped back into the kitchen and shut the door behind him. "Delfyne," he said.

She turned in a swirl of white.

"So…what *are* you doing exactly?" he asked, now that they were alone.

"I told you," she said. "Everything. It occurred to me that here, in this place away from everything and everyone I know, I can try things I've never had a chance to try. Here, not a soul other than you and my guards knows who I am, and they're posing as working guests on a ranch vacation. So, I'm anonymous. I'm free. At home no one lets me near the kitchen, but here I can do anything. Still, I'm really sorry I upset Lydia. I didn't mean to make a mess."

He shook his head. "Lydia's not upset about the mess. She just feels she's being a bad hostess."

Delfyne frowned. "Oh, no. Lydia is a fine hostess. I practically forced my way in here—I guess I do have a tendency to be imperious—and what was she to do? She's a love even to let me in her kitchen. Just look what I did!"

She held out both arms. They and her clothing were coated in white. Without thinking Owen reached out and traced a finger down the inside of one arm, leaving a trail of soft pink skin and revealing the delicate blue veins in her wrist.

A visible shiver went through her and he abruptly pulled back.

"What were you making?"

She glanced to the side. "There's the problem. I don't even know. In fact, I have absolutely no idea where a complete novice like me starts, but flour seemed a good idea. Don't most things have flour in them?" she asked, looking up at him as if she genuinely expected him to know.

For some reason he couldn't explain, he wished he could answer her question. Her eagerness was so charming that he wanted to be the one to show her the ropes, to be privy to that delicious enthusiasm. He wanted to lick chocolate frosting from her fingertips…

"Lydia is going to help you," he said, his voice rough. "She'll teach you."

Delfyne leaned back and looked up. "What did you say to her? You didn't order her to help me, did you? I don't want people to spend time with me out of obligation. There's always so much of that in my life. Even you—"

"No." The word came out harsher than he had intended. "I'll admit that I wasn't enthusiastic when Andreus approached me, and there are reasons why I still don't think it's the best idea in the world…"

"You think I'm a pest."

"I think you're a distraction. You're very beautiful."

"Distracting to…you?" Her eyes were wide.

"And pretty much any male in your vicinity."

"But you're implying that I'm no longer an obligation. Why?"

He glanced to the side. "I like you."

When he turned back she was beaming. "I don't think anyone has ever said that to me before."

"I don't believe that."

"No, it's true. When you're a—" she glanced around "—a you-know-what, people do things with you because they have to or because they think you can get something for them. Liking doesn't have anything to do with it. I like you, too. You didn't yell at Lydia, and your men respect you. You let me stay here and now you're giving me free access to your kitchen."

That elicited a laugh from him. "You could go anywhere you wanted to," he began, but then he stopped. That wasn't true. That was the reason she was here, because she *couldn't* go anywhere. She wasn't safe anywhere. And maybe not even here, with a man who found that her smile made him burn…

He wasn't going to do anything that might bring harm or pain or disgust to her life. He should get smart, go into town and hook up with one of the female sometime friends he knew. He definitely needed to bank the fire this woman had fanned to life within him. Yeah, he was going to do that real soon. And, as for Delfyne…

"Do *not* try to light that old gas stove again. We don't usually use it, and only Lydia understands it. She'll help you."

"I'll listen to her carefully," she promised. "And one day I'm going to serve you something that I made with my own hands. It will be a treat."

"I'll consider it as such."

She laughed, a sound that made him want to lean closer. "I meant *me*. It will be a treat for *me* to be able to say that I actually made something. I've never made anything in my life."

Suddenly she rose on her toes and kissed Owen on the cheek.

Like a torch filled with fuel, his senses burst into flame. Carefully he held himself in check, not following through on his impulse to turn so that his lips met hers, his warmth against her warmth, his mouth covering her mouth.

"I'll look forward to whatever you give me," he said, his voice brusque.

"And you'll be honest with me about how it tastes?" she asked.

Again he thought of her lips and how *she* would taste.

"I'll do that," he promised.

Later, when he stood outside beneath the stars thinking about the fact that Delfyne slept in one of his beds upstairs, he reminded himself that her glow, her enthusiasm, the way her whole body seemed barely to keep her spirit locked inside was simply the result of the newness of this experience.

To him this was home, a place he'd lived all his life. It wasn't exactly ordinary, but it was familiar. When the ranch became familiar to Delfyne, the new would have worn off, the enthusiasm would be gone.

Then she would see the rough parts, the lonely parts, the lack of things she was used to and wanted and she would look forward to leaving. That was the way it was with people who were brought or sent here rather than coming of their own accord.

Not that any of that mattered. She wouldn't be here long enough for that to happen. She had a prince waiting for her somewhere. By this time next year she would be married to him and in his bed.

Owen let his breath out in a whoosh, shook his head and moved farther away from the house. He wished the summer would end soon. Andreus owed him more than the man would ever know.

It was a debt he would never claim. Once this summer was over, it would probably be a good idea to break ties with his friend.

Andreus was a busy man.

And so am I, Owen thought. Tons of jobs to do around here. He intended to throw himself into work. No more stroking the new cook.

Delfyne looked at the massive four-poster bed where she had just finished changing the sheets. The bed was constructed from some sort of rustic golden wood, and it was Owen's. Lydia had said so while Delfyne was trailing her about, asking her to show her how to do all the hundreds of things that Lydia did every day.

She smoothed her palms over the green-and-blue quilt. It was the color of Montana, Lydia had said. Delfyne smiled. Lydia was always saying things like that, giving Delfyne a running commentary about this place and the people she so clearly loved. Except for Owen. She didn't say much about Owen.

"He's private," Lydia had told Delfyne. "He's a good man, but he's a hard man and he wouldn't like it if I talked about him, so I don't." Her words were clearly a warning, especially since Delfyne had been asking nonstop questions about anything and everything, especially Owen.

"I have to run out for a while, dear," Lydia said. "One morning a week, I deliver meals to shut-ins. Will you be all right here by yourself?"

"Oh yes, I have tons of things to do," Delfyne said, even though that wasn't really true. There was no sense in making Lydia feel bad for doing the things she needed to do or to make her feel that Delfyne was dependent on her for company and guidance, even though she was.

"You go. I have plans," Delfyne said, whirling from the bed. Her bracelets rattled as she moved, and Lydia frowned.

"When we make bread this afternoon, you'll have to take those off. You'll get them caught on the mixer and hurt yourself. They're not real practical for a ranch."

"I know, but I love them. I'm a sucker for inexpensive trinkets," she said, holding up her wrist with the silver, pink and lilac hearts dangling down. "I've been collecting them for a long time." Princesses didn't wear cheap jewelry in public. It was a total shame, in Delfyne's eyes.

"Go before I change my mind," she ordered Lydia, using the tone and words Lydia often used with her and ending on a laugh that made the older woman smile.

"Where on earth did Owen find a delightful fairy woman like you? You're nothing at all like the women he usually hangs around with," Lydia said, which made Delfyne's eyebrows rise.

"You're right. Forget I said that. Owen's taste is none of my concern, and I know that you're not one of his women. Both of you have told me already, you're the sister of an old college friend and you're from the east. But, sweetie, much as I adore you already, you clearly have never done manual labor, so don't try to do too much while I'm gone. And, Delfyne, don't—"

"Light the stove," Delfyne said before Lydia could finish. "I won't. That stove hates me."

"Stupid stove," Lydia said with a laugh.

When Lydia had gone, Delfyne tried to figure out something to do. What did ordinary women do with their time in situations like this? she wondered. What would Lydia do?

Lydia would clean, of course. But then Lydia was so good at her job that there was really nothing much left in the cleaning department for Delfyne to sink her teeth into.

"Except for the guest rooms that no one is staying in." Delfyne said the words out loud and immediately ran to get some supplies. What did she need? What did Lydia use?

A broom, a vacuum cleaner, some of those citrusy-smelling green cleaners Lydia seemed to favor. Maybe a bucket and some rags and a brush and…

Within minutes Delfyne was hard at work scrubbing bathrooms and polishing mirrors, sloshing water and swinging a broom around.

"What are you doing?" That low, deep voice caught her in midswing with her broom, and Delfyne jumped and whirled around. Dust swirled with her and she stepped in the dirt she had been trying to sweep up. She sneezed.

Owen was leaning against the door frame, regarding her with those lazy blue eyes that seemed to see the things she kept hidden inside. He was also looking at her as if…

She followed the path his gaze had taken and realized that her blouse was torn. It was a small tear, one she'd dismissed as insignificant when it had happened. Certainly not much of her skin was revealed. But Owen had noticed. Her body tightened with awareness and her breath hitched in an alarming way.

"I'm—I'm sweeping," she said.

"I see that. But maybe I should have rephrased that question. *Why* are you sweeping?"

"I'm learning."

"I pay Lydia to clean."

Delfyne frowned. "Lydia didn't tell me to do this. She isn't trying to get out of work."

"I didn't say that she was. In fact, I would never accuse her of something like that, so…is it important for you to know how to sweep?"

"It's important for me to live, really live and to see how others live. To experience things I haven't experienced."

"But not to damage yourself."

"I'm not damaged."

"You sneezed. Maybe you're allergic to the damn dirt for all I know. Probably for all you know, too. I don't like the feeling that we're acting like the ugly stepsisters and treating you like Cinderella among the cinders. I'll bet you haven't spent much time playing in the dirt."

She couldn't help laughing then. He sounded so chagrined.

"Maybe I missed out on a lot being a princess. You should go. I'm only on my second room and there are a lot more to do."

He looked around the room, which was, Delfyne was delighted to realize, sparkling, even if the bedspread was hanging a bit crooked.

"I cleaned the bathroom, too," she pointed out. "All by myself."

He grinned then. "You don't say."

"I do say."

"For a princess you're quite a surprise."

She laughed again. "You know a lot of princesses?"

"What do you think?"

"I don't know. Andreus tells me that you're very wealthy. You could travel in higher circles if you wanted. I know some princesses who would definitely be interested in catching your eye."

He raised a brow and an unfamiliar sense of warmth crept up her spine and her face.

"You're blushing, Delfyne."

"No, I'm not. Princesses don't."

"All right." He shrugged. "You've done a fine job here," he said, motioning to the room.

"Thank you."

"But I think you've done enough."

Delfyne tilted her head, confused. "Did I do something wrong?"

"No, I did. I let this get out of hand. You were supposed to be having a little fun, not laboring, and I… You ripped your blouse."

"It's a very small tear."

"But that's a pretty blouse. You're not used to this kind of thing."

"You just said I did a good job."

"And you did, but…I just got through talking to Alice, Ennis's wife. She told me she spoke with Lydia when Lydia was leaving the ranch."

"Yes. Lydia had a task to do."

"I know that, but—"

"But what?" Delfyne wondered why Owen looked so perturbed.

He said something beneath his breath that she couldn't make out. "Alice tells me I'm being a very bad host. She said I've never treated a guest so badly before."

Delfyne's eyes opened wide. "Why did she say that?"

"Because…she's right, you know. You've been here for days, and I've kept you a virtual prisoner in the house."

"You don't have to explain. I know that I tend to stand out. All your employees look at me as if they wonder who I really am. I suppose you don't often have totally unexplained guests who stay the whole summer."

Owen frowned. "I don't want you to worry about that. My employees might wonder about you, but they'd never talk about you. They're loyal."

"But not everyone in town would be loyal. They would ask a

lot of questions that might be tricky to answer. I know I don't exactly look or sound as if I'm an American."

"So…you don't want me to take you to visit the town as Alice suggested?"

Delfyne's heart leaped. She *did* want to go to town, but Owen was beating himself up for not having seen that. This Alice woman had criticized him and made him seem like a bad host. For some reason, that made Delfyne angry, even though the woman had been taking her side.

"I'm perfectly fine," Delfyne lied. But she could see by the look in Owen's eyes that he didn't believe her.

"Let's go," he said.

"Go where?"

"Out. Lunch. With Lydia gone, I'll bet you haven't eaten."

But then she would be sitting across from him, staring into those amazing eyes and looking at that chest and those shoulders and listening to the deep timbre of his voice, which gave her shivers and made her susceptible and…she hated being susceptible. Being susceptible had resulted in too many very bad and regrettable, humiliating experiences. That just wasn't going to happen, especially not with a man who could cause her so much heartache and regret. She so didn't want this time in her life to be about regret or to end badly.

Despite her desire to see the sights, there was no question that going out with Owen could be dangerous. She had to protect herself from making another horrible mistake. Instantly, Delfyne went into full princess mode, standing taller, staring directly into Owen's eyes, her chin tilted slightly. "I'm sorry. I can't possibly oblige you by leaving now. I'm not finished here yet."

He grinned, a strong, full grin that made her toes curl. "We'll compromise. I'll wait. I'll give you time to finish this room and then we're going." He started to leave.

"Wait. I haven't said yes yet." She crossed her arms and frowned.

"Say yes." Owen turned and stared at her dead-on, and all that masculine energy, that…edge that was such an intriguing part of him seemed to wrap around her and lay waste to every ounce of common sense and willpower she possessed.

Oh, she wanted to say yes, badly. But she clutched her broom and tilted her chin higher. "I'm not Ennis or Len," she said.

His answering smile was slow, his amusement evident. "No question of that." They stood silently for maybe five seconds. Not long at all, but every second seemed like forever in the presence of this man who radiated such virility. Then, just when she thought he was going to go away, just when she thought she could start breathing normally again and stop thinking about words like *virility*, he gave her a slight, terse nod of his head. "Please. Say yes, Delfyne," he added, and she got the feeling that *please* wasn't a word he used often or with ease. The fact that he had made the effort melted something in her that she didn't want to melt.

"Maybe," she said.

"Stubborn."

Now she smiled. "I'm taking time off from having my life ordered for me."

Immediately he turned sober. "You're right. You're my guest, and even if you weren't…it's not my place to order you around."

He turned to leave. She had won. She also realized what he had offered and she had turned down. A chance to go out and see the town. People. Sights. The chance to appear in public as an ordinary person, not a royal.

Running after him, broom still in hand, Delfyne reached the top of the stairs. "Owen?"

He turned and looked up at her. And waited.

"I'll be ready in fifteen minutes. I'm a little wet," she said, looking down at the way her blouse was plastered to her skin from cleaning the bathroom.

"I noticed." His gaze darkened. "Wet looks good on you."

She shivered inside but managed to maintain a cool facade. At least she hoped she did. "That's a compliment?"

"That's a fact. Probably one I shouldn't have mentioned."

But he had, she thought as he strode away, and now her heart was thudding with anticipation. She was going to town with Owen. As a regular woman, not as a princess.

She fully intended to make the most of the situation.

CHAPTER FIVE

THE woman was getting under his skin and having an unwanted effect on him. No doubt about that, Owen thought. They'd been halfway to the town of Bigsby when he'd realized he had whisked her away without so much as a word to Nicholas and Theron.

"It won't be a problem as long as we're not gone too long," Delfyne had said. "I told them I needed a little privacy, so they've retreated to the bunkhouse for a couple of hours. We can't go out in public with a telltale entourage."

So…the clock was ticking, Owen realized as he ushered her into the Molly and Me restaurant in the town of Bigsby.

Immediately, heads turned and people called out greetings.

"It's been too long since you came in, Owen," the owner of the restaurant said. Molly was wearing her customary white blouse and black skirt. She looked severe as always, until she turned to Delfyne and smiled. "And I see you brought a guest. An elegant lady guest." Molly turned to him expectantly.

Of course, her comments were really questions, and Owen wanted to groan. Not that he hadn't prepared himself for the inevitable curiosity.

Out of the corner of his eye he could see dismay on Delfyne's face. "Elegant?" she said. Owen could practically see the wheels turning behind those pretty eyes. *I can't let her know I'm a princess* was what Delfyne was probably thinking.

Molly looked perplexed. "I was talking about your shoes."

Delfyne leaned back and looked down to the pretty little bits of beige on her feet. He could almost feel her dismay that she had been betrayed by a pair of shoes that he was pretty sure Delfyne thought of as plain and unrevealing. Probably a lot of other people would have thought the same thing. But Molly? She noticed things and she knew things.

"My…shoes?" Delfyne asked, and he would bet that she was stalling for time.

Molly looked at Owen with suspicion, as if he had started dating an unworthy woman or at least one who didn't understand the English language. "Angel, this is Montana, not Antarctica. I may dress plain for work but I know my shoes. Those are Manolos. That spells elegance in my book."

Suddenly Delfyne looked up and laughed, a trace of impishness in her expression. "I see. Yes, I got these from someone who has a lot of money to spend but not much use for exotic clothes right now."

That elicited a smile from Molly. "Lucky you."

"I think so. I'm Delfyne, by the way."

"Unusual name. Pretty. Owen, I didn't know you had a guest. In fact, I don't remember you ever having a woman guest. You're always hosting cattlemen and stockbrokers, and they've all been male."

Great. The tone of Molly's voice sent her message loud and clear. She thought he and Delfyne were romantically linked and she would make it her business to discover all of the details.

"Oh, I'm not the usual kind of guest," Delfyne said suddenly. "I've been helping Lydia out."

"You're helping Lydia? Lydia, who more or less raised Owen

along with her own three kids, ran a house and worked full-time while working part-time for the Second Chance? Lydia, who has probably not taken more than one day a week off and one vacation week a year since her husband died five years ago when she started running Owen's household full-time?"

Delfyne gave Owen a critical look. "One week a year? Owen, it's very important to treat those who work for you with respect and empathy. One week is not possibly enough."

Owen felt a small headache forming between his eyes. He wondered if Delfyne knew how regal she sounded and looked when she got that snooty, pretty, sexy, disapproving tilt to her head and that unbending velvet tone to her voice.

He forced a small smile. "Ladies, I've tried to get Lydia to take more time off. Believe me."

"Oh. You have? That's wonderful." Delfyne looked as if he had just given her a gift. "In that case, please forget I lectured you. You're a good employer."

Molly was looking more confused than ever at the employee who had lectured her employer. "So, Delfyne, you said you're helping Lydia? Forgive me for being nosy, but…why? And how? And how did this come about? How did Owen end up hiring you? You're definitely not from around here."

Uh-oh. Molly was just getting started. It wasn't going to matter if Delfyne had royal training. She would be no match if Molly wanted answers. The woman knew how to get her way. Like it or not, he was going to have to wade into this, Owen knew.

He cleared his throat. "Regarding Lydia, let's just say that someone brought it to my attention that it's important to live a little. It's probably good for Lydia to have a spare moment or two," he said, trying to skirt an actual lie and ignoring half of Molly's questions. He hated dishonest people.

"So…you thought Lydia needed help and you hired

Delfyne here." Molly shook her head as she studied Delfyne head to toe.

"Oh, I'm *not* hired," Delfyne said. "I'm just an ordinary person in need of a place to stay who wanted to experience the Second Chance and your Montana. Owen agreed to let me visit and help out a little. I think you call those working vacations, don't you? The ones where you get to experience ranch life and also do some good? I so hope I'll be a credit to the Second Chance. I hear that Owen has lots of guests sometimes, and Lydia has all those rooms to clean and…"

Delfyne left her sentence hanging.

Slowly, Molly nodded. "Yes, I guess you're right. I wouldn't want to have to handle a crowd at the ranch all by myself. It's good of you to help Lydia. Nice to meet you, Delfyne. So…how did you hook up with Owen?"

Molly glanced down at Delfyne's shoes again. Owen was sure Molly had a million questions about Delfyne, but the working vacation wasn't a bad story. It was certainly more believable than the truth—that Owen had been asked to be knight errant for a princess who had been banished to Montana and the Second Chance for the summer.

"Oh, my brother knows him from college." Delfyne gave Molly a pitiful glance. "You must think Owen is getting a very poor deal having me as a helper, don't you? I know I don't look very useful, and I do have my limitations. I'm quite good at cleaning things, but not so very handy with a stove yet. I haven't eaten since breakfast, so after I spent the morning scrubbing rooms, I guess Owen thought I needed sustenance, and with Lydia out…"

Delfyne held out her hands in dismissal.

Sustenance? Inwardly, Owen groaned, but he couldn't let it show. It was, in his mind, unbelievable that Delfyne was spinning this ridiculous tale and Molly was buying into it. Besides the expensive shoes and clothes, the very tilt of Delfyne's head, her accent, the way she enunciated her words and looked around the room as if she were surveying her domain practically shouted breeding to Owen. But while the men in the room were giving Delfyne surreptitious appreciative looks and the women were studying her as if she were a new rival come to town, none of them seemed to see anything out of the ordinary other than her obvious beauty.

Except Molly still seemed to be fixating on those shoes. "Well, of course, you needed food and Owen brought you to just the right place to get a decent meal. Those shoes are just so…perfect," she said. Owen knew how Molly's mind worked. She was probably estimating the cost of the shoes and wondering who Delfyne had gotten them from.

"Molly, are you listening? We need food, not shoes. Just look at this woman," Owen said suddenly. "The merest breeze will blow her over. She worked like a dog this morning. She needs feeding. Soon."

It was perhaps unfair, but Owen knew Molly's hot-button issues. Food ranked right at the top. Immediately she seemed to forget everything that they had been discussing, including Delfyne's designer shoes.

"Oh, you're right. Just look at you, you little thing," Molly agreed, patting Delfyne's hand. "You're gorgeous, of course, and tall, but so slender. And there's lots of hard work on Owen's ranch. All those rooms. No wonder Owen decided that Lydia needs some help. Lyd's not as young as she once was even if she won't admit it. We all have to slow down and give the young blood a chance to do their part and she's no different than the rest of us. Now you just wait there. I'll get you something that will fill you up and get you through the rest of the day."

She seated them at a table and when she had gone, Owen leaned over and, keeping his voice low, said, "I'm sorry. I shouldn't have brought you here."

The look in her eyes was incredulous. "Are you kidding? This is marvelous! Molly thinks I'm a real person."

"You *are* a real person."

"I know. She thinks I'm a real *regular* person."

Owen sincerely doubted that, but Delfyne was smiling so brightly that he wasn't about to spoil things for her.

A low, rumbling sound intruded, the clearing of a gravelly throat. "Owen, we've been patient. We waited our turn. Now come on and introduce us to the lady," someone next to Owen's elbow said. Owen turned around to see a crowd of older men he had known most of his life. Friends of his father's and now friends of his. They were smiling and preening like a bunch of peacocks. And Owen noticed that Dave Ollington—not an older man but a young and handsome one—was part of their group. Dave wasn't preening. He was positively salivating.

Immediately Owen shifted, blocking part of Dave's view.

"The lady—" Owen began.

"I'm Delfyne, a visitor and house help at the ranch," she said with a smile.

"House help?" one of the men said. "Does that mean Lydia finally has some time on her hands?"

Owen did a double take at the interest in Ben Whitcliff's voice. Lydia was a widow. To Owen, she was practically family, but he had no idea what her social life consisted of. Did she date? Did she *want* to date?

"Oh, yes, I'm sure Lydia has time on her hands," Delfyne was saying to Ben. "Or, at least, I intend to make sure she has some. Owen feels the same, don't you?"

He fought to hold back his grin. He wondered if she had any

idea that most maids didn't call their employers by their first names and treat them like old friends. Maybe she thought people in small towns who weren't royalty operated under different rules with the hired help. Or maybe the princess beneath the maid was struggling to stay locked away.

"I'll make sure Lydia has enough time off to do whatever she wants and needs to do," he said.

"I'm going to work extra hard to help her with the house," Delfyne added. "That's going to be so much fun."

Dave chuckled. "You are absolutely charming, Delfyne."

She smiled at the handsome man and Owen had a ridiculous urge to dig his elbow into Dave's stomach. Hard. "Thank you," Delfyne said.

"You never took *Lydia* out to lunch," Harlan Bonnet noted.

Delfyne opened her mouth and Owen just knew that she was going to declare that he would be taking Lydia out from now on. The woman certainly knew how to issue decrees.

"Delfyne's new to town," Owen said, trying to avoid trouble. "Now and then she'll have to run errands for Lydia, so she needs to know where everything is," he added. It was sort of the truth.

At that moment a waitress delivered their food, and the group began to slowly shuffle away. "So…where did you say you were from, sweet thing?" Dave asked.

Immediately, Delfyne turned. The smile was gone from her face and she looked troubled.

"Her name's not sweet thing," Owen warned. "And she's under my care. Remember that. I'll expect you to respect my—"

My what? Owen thought. What had Delfyne told Molly she was? Both a guest and an employee? It was only a small lie and yet…already this crazy situation had him lying, or at least hiding the truth. Anger sliced through him. Too much of his life had been ruined by lies and expectations that couldn't be met.

Dave looked more than a little miffed. "I wasn't trying to be disrespectful, Owen. I was being interested. Everyone knows that you're not interested in relationships, so you don't have anything to offer a woman, but some of us do."

Which was a total crock. Dave had never offered a woman more than a few months of fun as far as Owen could tell, but he wasn't going to trade relationship stories with Dave, now or ever, especially since that would only draw attention to Delfyne and start a buzz that might never die down.

He ignored Dave until the man went away. Then he and Delfyne ate their meal in silence. When they left the restaurant she asked if she could take a minute to buy shoes.

His eyes opened wide. "Shoes? You want to go shoe shopping in Bigsby?" For certain there weren't any stores that sold designer shoes here. And if she asked for them…

"Don't look at me that way," she said.

"What way?"

"The way Andreus does sometimes. As if I'm about to do something foolish. I'm not. I'm not asking to do something frivolous. These shoes are obviously all wrong and not sensible enough if they attract so much attention. And I'll be quick. I promise. I just—I *do* need shoes and I haven't seen anything at all of the town since I've been here. Just fifteen minutes, please."

Immediately, Owen felt like a jerk. She had been sent here for what was to have been the trip of a lifetime and now some clueless, grumpy rancher was begrudging her even a short trip to look for shoes she really needed. He'd been so concerned that something would happen to her and that he'd betray his friend's trust in him that he'd been keeping her a virtual prisoner. What kind of man did that?

But he knew. He'd already been that man, just like his father before him, or so his wife had said. She'd hated the ranch and even the town and there had been no escaping what her perceived imprisonment on the ranch had done to their relationship. Now she was gone, and he was here with his ghosts. But none of that was Delfyne's fault or her problem.

"I'd like to let you have more freedom," Owen began, "but—"

"You think some man like that odious one will accost me."

He smiled. "Somehow I don't think any of the women around here have ever called Dave odious." But then, those women weren't princesses with princes coming to call. Delfyne was used to more elegant, handsome, wealthy and privileged men than Dave paying attention to her.

"And no," he continued. "I doubt even Dave would do anything too offensive in broad daylight. I just don't want anyone to corner you and ask you a lot of personal questions, which they're sure to do. Word travels fast, and the fact that I now apparently have a guest-helper who could model in *Vogue* is bound to cause a stir. There aren't many women who look like you around here. And there are absolutely none with the air that surrounds you."

She bit her lip. "I'll try to look more common."

Oh, that was too amusing. He wanted to caress her cheek when he gave her the bad news that she would never look common no matter what she did, but touching her was a bad idea on too many fronts even to think about. Especially touching her right here where everyone could see.

"Just be yourself," he said. "You'll be fine." He would make sure that no one ruined things for her. "Now, let's go get those shoes. And you take as much time as you want. We'll take the long way around so you can see all of the town."

She smiled up at him as if he had given her the keys to the kingdom. Her eyes lit up, and, as he led her down the street past shops he had seen thousands of times in his lifetime, she turned and looked at each one as if she'd never seen a store before.

"What's that?" she asked.

"Feed and seed. I guess you've never been in one of those before."

She laughed. "I've never even been in a diner before today. It was fun, and I adore Molly, but—" Suddenly her hand was on his arm, her fingertips light and delicate, her touch feeling far too good. Owen's whole body reacted. "I'm sorry you had to lie about me. And I dragged you into this. I wish I could be more honest," she said, and he knew she was telling the truth. What must it be like to have to be followed around by a phalanx of bodyguards all the time?

And of course her men would be missing her soon.

"I can handle a little dishonesty when it's for the right cause," he said. "And I wouldn't forgive myself if I let anything happen to you. The truth might open you to danger."

But as they stood in the street, her skin against his, Owen knew that there were other dangers here that he didn't want to think about, other temptations, other mistakes that could be made but never recalled once they were out of the box.

"I'd better get you to the store and back to the ranch," he said. "Lydia is going to be worried." Another half truth. Lydia would assume that Delfyne was safe with him, and she'd be half right. His thoughts might be in the wrong place, but so far he was controlling his body. Barely.

Still, his comment about Lydia had apparently cast a pall on Delfyne's fun. Within a half hour, Delfyne had shoes, a pair of boots and some jeans and white shirts. Owen had rushed in at just the right moment to witness Delfyne's distressed look. He realized the problem. She didn't have any way to pay. He supposed that princesses didn't carry cash around on them.

"Bill them to the Second Chance," he told the clerk.

"Thank you. You will, of course, be repaid in full for all you've done," Delfyne said in that every-inch-the-princess tone.

Owen's gaze and the clerk's locked. If the man had been the sort to ask nosy questions of his customers, Delfyne's last line might have elicited a few. As it was, Owen was the one asking questions of himself. What *was* he doing?

He was lying, going along with this charade and acting crazy because of a woman…again.

The acting crazy had to stop right now. He knew all the facts, and he wasn't dumb enough to fall for a woman he couldn't have and definitely couldn't hold. Not this time.

CHAPTER SIX

DELFYNE rushed up to Owen the next morning, her arms out to the sides. "Do I finally look the part now? I dare anyone to mistake me for a princess like this."

She was dressed in a plain white blouse, open at the neck, and a pair of blue jeans that clung to her curves like icing on a cake.

Heat sizzled through him, but he pushed it aside. She wasn't asking what her jeans did to his temperature.

"You look like a woman who means business," he said.

"And I do. Today, Lydia's letting me back in the kitchen. We're baking cookies. I'll bring you some when they're done. And then Morgan is going to show me how to milk a cow. Isn't that exciting? That is, we have cows, of course, in Xenora, but no one has ever suggested that I might milk one."

"I'll just bet they haven't," Owen said with a grin.

She wrinkled her nose. "Make fun of me if you will, but you haven't spent your life in a pretty box."

He studied her. She was right. He had lived his life on his own terms and done exactly what he wanted to, when he wanted to, where he wanted to, with disastrous consequences for those closest to him.

"Is your pretty box that bad?"

She gazed up at him, her eyes bright and earnest. "No, it's not.

I know how privileged I am, but…I've been impetuous at times. Always. I never walked. I ran. I never trotted sedately. I galloped. And sometimes I did things and said things that were so spontaneous and ill-thought-out that I scared those I love. There are things even beyond what they know…things I've done that I regret, and I—I guess I see why they've tried to hem me in, but it's so very hard not to want to experience things. I know they're not trying to punish me, but…oh, I'm saying this badly, I know."

But she wasn't. Not really. Owen stepped closer. "Do you feel trapped here at the Second Chance?" He'd heard that before.

She looked at him sharply and he knew that she had heard about his wife. Not a surprise, even though he knew that Andreus wouldn't have shared much even with his family. Faye had cried to pretty much everyone who would listen before she left him. *Trapped* had been one of the nicer words she'd used. And later…everything had spiraled out of control after their tragedy.

"You've been completely hospitable to me," she said. "How could I feel trapped? How could I be so ungrateful?"

That soft, silky voice washed over him, and frustration rushed through him.

"You don't have to be grateful. I don't want your gratitude. I know all too well that a trip to Bigsby and the Second Chance wasn't a part of your plans."

"And I know all too well that having a princess disrupt your life and the sanctity of your calm household wasn't a part of your plans, either. Andreus asked a lot of you."

"Andreus could ask for whatever he wanted, and I would give it."

Delfyne studied him. "I—as a sister who loves her brother, I'm grateful to hear that. Andreus and you…I know your friendship dates back to college, but such loyalty as that…to offer everything—"

"Don't make it out to be something noble. I owe Andreus."

"Why?"

Even if she hadn't said it, the question in her eyes let Owen know that she didn't understand what he was talking about, and why should she? Andreus wouldn't have spilled Owen's secrets. Realizing that he had said too much, Owen turned away. Despite his friendship with her brother—and partly because of the friendship—he couldn't get too personal with Delfyne. Exposing himself to that kind of risk when the barriers that separated them were so impassable… He'd have to be ten kinds of foolish to go there.

"I'd better get to work," he said. But work wasn't the reason he was running. There were so many reasons. The woman he shouldn't be tempted by, the memory of his son's tragic death, which still brought him to his knees, and…he didn't want to talk about what had happened to forge an unbreakable bond between himself and her brother. He didn't want to remember, and he didn't want to see pity in Delfyne's eyes. That was more than a man could take.

He strode toward the door as if he could chase down his problems and conquer them if only he moved fast enough.

"You've done it again, you fool," Delfyne muttered to herself after Owen had gone. "Always just rushing in without thinking about what you're doing."

Owen had opened his house to her. He'd inconvenienced himself and he'd allowed her to lead him into lies she knew he hadn't wanted to tell. He had been the perfect host, but she had not been the perfect guest. Even if she hadn't spoken her questions out loud, her curiosity had been clear by her tone and her demeanor. She'd stepped over a line.

Not that she hadn't stepped over lines before, but this time, her reason was unnerving. Owen fascinated her. He was so obviously strong, a leader, a respected man of the community, and yet despite that strength, that air of machismo, he'd allowed her to mess up his kitchen. He'd played along with her playacting. There had not been one word about her duty.

That was heady stuff for someone like her. She had let it go to her head, and she'd wanted to know more about him even though keeping a barrier was the smart thing to do. Owen obviously wanted that barrier, too. She owed him an apology for even thinking about breaching his privacy.

But it soon became apparent that she wouldn't be able to apologize. Owen didn't come near the house all day. And night fell without his return.

Lying in the inky darkness at three in the morning, tossing in her bed, Delfyne knew she had to make amends, to apologize for pushing Owen.

So, long before dawn, Delfyne arose, pulled on clothing and waited for Owen. The minute she heard him moving around, she went to his door and knocked.

When he pulled open the door, he was wearing jeans and no shirt, as if he'd rushed to answer her knock, and he looked worried. She realized probably no one sought him out this early unless there was a problem, so she held up one hand.

"Nothing's wrong," she said quickly. "That is, I just wanted to apologize, to tell you I'm sorry about trying to wheedle out information about your relationship with my brother yesterday and also…about everything. I'm sure this whole experience has been an irritation, to say the least, and definitely an imposition. You've been a wonderful host. I'm grateful, and I won't push again."

She was intensely aware of his naked chest, of the fact that he towered over her and of those fierce, silver-blue eyes that seemed to see things—her fears and insecurities—that she had always tried to hide.

"You didn't do anything wrong," he said in that deep voice that thrilled her against her better judgment.

"I asked you for personal information you hadn't offered. That's an invasion of your privacy. And no one knows more than I how important privacy is. Yet I prodded you when you've been nothing but kind to me."

Owen muttered something that sounded like a curse, turned and grabbed a white shirt, shrugged into it and took her by the hand. "Come on."

"Where are we going?"

"To talk. Somewhere we won't be interrupted by anyone." His tone was brusque. He was frowning.

"You're still angry." She couldn't keep the sadness from her voice. "Princesses—well, we lead privileged lives and we take a lot for granted. That's not a good thing. I suppose I'm not very good at apologies."

"Don't say another word." He kept moving, his large hand hard and strong where it cupped her own. When they were out of the house, he kept walking until they were in a copse of trees beside a stream. A very large rock with an indentation in the center sat next to the water as if it had been placed there.

"Sit down," he told her.

She sat, as if he were the prince and she the commoner. She waited. He faced her.

"I'm the one who owes you an apology," he said.

"No, I—"

"Delfyne." His voice was weary. "Let me finish. You were right about me being angry, but I wasn't mad at you. I was upset about a lot of things, but none of it was your fault."

"The nosy question was definitely my fault," she said.

A low laugh escaped him.

"What did I say?" she asked, wondering how she could make him laugh like that again.

"It's not the question, Princess, it's the tone. The way you speak, all haughty and royal, as if your word is the last word."

"Well," she said with a small, guilty smile. "It often is."

"I know that. I'm very aware of your rank...always."

"My rank—it means I get my way too often. You still haven't accepted my apology. Rank is no excuse for bad manners or prying."

He held out his hand. "Andreus is your brother, and he's put you in my hands because he trusts me. You deserve to know why he trusts me so much."

"You're friends. You're close."

"It's more than that. I meant what I said when I told you that he had the right to ask anything he wanted of me. You—this arrangement—it's more than unusual. It's extreme in its own way. That is...I'm sure anyone in the kind of situation you and Andreus and your other family members are in often have to elude the public for safety's sake, but it's all new to me. Yet I fell into line, because Andreus went to the mat for me. You know that expression?"

She shook her head.

"It's when one person supports another person with no reservations. There was a time in my life when I was in danger of losing it completely, and Andreus came to my rescue. He dropped everything—I'm sure that was no mean feat—and he flew here, listened to me and stuck by me until I could function again. It wouldn't be out of line to say that he saved me from self-destruction. That's why he can ask whatever he likes."

Owen's words were matter-of-fact, but the look in his eyes was so intense—the memories were clearly causing him pain, but he wasn't shying away—that Delfyne felt her throat closing up.

"You don't have to tell me anything."

"I should have told you already. Andreus probably wanted to, but he held back out of respect for my privacy. That wasn't fair. It might have helped both of you if the truth came out. You should know what your brother has done for me. I'll tell you…if that's all right with you?"

Delfyne fought the lump in her throat. She nodded.

"All right. Tell me what you know already and I'll fill in the blanks." Then he sat down beside her and waited.

There were inches separating him from Delfyne, but Owen instantly became aware of her nearness and of his error in sitting next to her. Tension filled his body, but he couldn't back down. They were both caught up in this impossible situation. It wasn't fair that she should be kept in the dark.

Besides, he was too attracted to her. If he told her what kind of man he really was, it would be one more barrier between them. He needed barriers. As many as he could manage.

"I know a little. A very little. I know you had a wife who didn't want to ranch. I know you had a child who died. And I know that you didn't want me here."

"Because a woman like you doesn't belong in a place like this."

"If it's such an awful place, why do you stay?"

He shook his head. "It's not an awful place. I love it, and for me it's the only place, but it's not where a woman like you is meant to be."

She stared at him. "A woman like me? Because I'm a princess?"

"Even if you weren't. This is a beautiful land, but at times it's harsh and demanding. The winters can be brutal. A ranch is like a mistress who eats up all of a man's time, even when that man has money."

"Did you deny her your time?"

"I left her alone too much, yes."

"That was bad."

In other circumstances her simple statement might have brought a smile to his face, but not this time. "It was. She was a woman who needed things. Light and company and fun and adoration and a much bigger world than this."

"And yet she married you."

"I think she thought we could compromise, that there would be more than there is. I thought so, too. At least I'm sure I gave her that impression, and she thought—because I have money—she thought I was a different kind of man than I actually am."

"Did you take her out on dates or things like that?"

"I took her on trips, but trips are short. They're not day-to-day. This is." He held his hands out and nodded toward the window and the empty expanses. "But I have to give her credit. She kept trying to get me to change, and I almost considered trying it her way and living somewhere else for a while, just to make her happy. Then James died. We buried him here, and she knew I'd never leave then. She thought I blamed her."

Delfyne looked up at him with big, dark eyes. "Did you?"

"Yes. I was on a business trip, and she was angry because I was on the road while she was stuck here in a place she hated. After she put James to bed, she called a friend, a former boyfriend, and because she felt guilty about that she went outside to talk so that she wouldn't be cheating in the same house where her baby was sleeping. So, neither of us was there when it happened. My son died in his bed alone, and though the doctors told us that there was no way we could have known or stopped it from happening, I blamed her. I blamed myself just as much. I blamed God and everyone and everything that came near me. My little boy died in the dark alone, so I put him in the ground on the land that my father and grandfather had made their own and I promised him that I'd never leave him alone again.

"I think it was even harder for her to be here then, living with the pain. She couldn't stay. I couldn't go. I think I would have gone insane and drunk myself to death if Andreus hadn't put his own life on hold and showed up to order me around until I was able to get a handle on things myself. So…that's how you came to be here."

"It's a hard story," she said simply.

"And not one I tell often."

She nodded solemnly. "Thank you for explaining to me. I understand more now. I see why Andreus chose this place and you."

"Because I owed him."

"No. Because you live with guilt because you think you failed to protect. So you won't let that happen again. You'll protect *me*." Then she stood up and kissed him on the cheek. Gently.

A rush of heat seared through him. "Don't do that. You may be right about my need to protect, but I'm not infallible. You're who you are."

She looked up, and he knew she was going to get all upset about him calling her out on being a princess. Without thought he placed two fingers over her lips. "You're who you are," he repeated. "You're a desirable woman. That makes me a dangerous man."

And he replaced his fingertips with his lips. For seconds he felt her cool perfect mouth beneath his own. He fought not to move or taste or take things further. This was just a warning…for both of them. No more.

Then he moved away. "I'm not the type of man who apologizes for kissing a desirable woman, either. Andreus might have trusted me too much. It would be best if we don't spend too much time together. Now you know all there is to know about me."

She looked shocked, dazed, and Owen walked away feeling as

if he had kicked a kitten. But no, that wasn't right, was it? He felt as if he had just kissed a woman he wanted to kiss again. And again.

Delfyne stood there, her fingertips pressed to her lips, and fought the urge to run after Owen.

Because he's still a man in pain and a man who's unfair to himself, she tried to tell herself. But she knew that wasn't the true reason, at least not all of it. She wanted him to kiss her again. And she saw right then and there how his wife had gotten caught in the snare of wanting something so badly that she'd convinced herself that what was wrong was right, that red was blue, that earth was sky.

Owen's wife had deceived herself into seeing what hadn't ever been there. And Delfyne had done that, too, several frightening times. The last time that had happened back at home…

She'd learned that cold, hard, painful lesson all too well. "Don't start seeing things that don't exist," she whispered to herself. "Because even if they do exist, this summer is just a moment, one that is going to end."

She didn't want to think about that, and the best way to keep from thinking was to keep busy. Delfyne turned to head off to the kitchen, but when she reached the hallway she ran smack into Theron and Nicholas, her bodyguards. They were looking at her as if she had just done something unholy.

One of them, Theron, looked at her clothes. "Not good quality," he said. "Does your family know that you're posing as a servant?"

She raised her chin. "My family knows that I'm safe."

"They *think* you're safe."

"What does that mean?"

He looked off in the direction Owen had gone.

Delfyne frowned. "Owen is my brother's dear friend."

"Yes, but…"

"What?"

"He looks at you as if he wants you."

She crossed her arms and rose to her fullest height, looking down at them. "Theron, you've guarded me a long time, you're as much friend as guard, but Owen is an honorable man. You have to know that."

"He seems that way, I've heard he's that way, but he's still a man. And you're…"

"I know who I am and I know what my future holds. You don't need to remind me of that. And…"

They waited.

"I wish you wouldn't follow me so closely. You don't do that at home. Why do it here?"

"You went to town without us the other day."

"I needed to. Your presence makes it too obvious what I am and I don't want anyone to know that."

Nicholas opened his mouth. To object, she was sure, so she rushed on. "Nicholas, look, please. No princess could ask for better bodyguards, but for once in my life, I want—I *need*—some personal space. No one even knows I'm here and *unless* someone realizes who I am—which isn't going to happen unless someone starts wondering why I have two hulking men trailing me about—nothing bad will happen to me." Unless her own foolish longing to feel Owen's lips against hers again led her to do something she'd end up regretting.

Nicholas shifted from one foot to another. "So, what should we do?"

Suddenly she felt an affinity for these men that she'd never felt before. They were as much at loose ends as she was. Ships out of water, hemmed in, not knowing what to do with themselves.

She shrugged. "What you've been doing. Whatever the ranch hands do. Find Owen or one of his workers and tell them you want to help more."

The men stood there for a minute as if she had suggested that they circumnavigate the globe while hopping on one foot.

"We should keep being ranchers?"

They exchanged looks, then turned to Delfyne. "Andreus might not like it."

She shook her head. "Andreus is thousands of miles away. He has no idea what it's like to twiddle his thumbs all day when there's work to be done. And I'm your princess. You're here to work for me. Go work. Go ranch. I'm telling you to do this thing. Are you going to ignore my request?"

In a matter of seconds the men had gone. Delfyne headed for the kitchen, where she hoped to forget the taste of Owen in a batch of cookie dough.

She was on her fourth batch—the first unburned batch—and Lydia was praising her for remembering that cookies quickly turned from tasty to torched in a matter of seconds if she didn't watch over them carefully when the telephone rang and Lydia turned to Delfyne.

"Will you be okay on your own?"

Indignation swirled through Delfyne even though she knew Lydia had excellent reasons for asking the question and even though Lydia had been patient and nurturing.

"I can do this," Delfyne assured her. "Go."

Lydia raised a brow and Delfyne realized that she had answered in full princess tone. "Please," she added gently.

The woman slipped out of the room and Delfyne turned to the oven, carefully opening it and sliding a cookie sheet out as Lydia had shown her.

She placed it on the stovetop and shut the oven door, then

picked up a spatula and removed a cookie, putting it on a cooling rack. Perfect.

Three more. Perfect.

One more.

"Those smell good."

She shrieked and the cookie fell off the spatula headed toward the floor. Delfyne lunged for it, then immediately jerked back as the hot cookie touched her fingers.

"Damn it," Owen said, marching forward and reaching for her hand.

"No. I'm fine," she said, trying to hide her hand behind her back.

"Let me see."

"No." She tried not to look distressed.

Owen stopped and stared at her. "I—are you afraid of me? Because I kissed you?"

No, she was afraid of herself, but she couldn't say that, and she couldn't let him think she feared him. Owen already had enough guilt to live with.

Slowly she pulled her hand from behind her and presented it to him.

Gently, he held her wrist between his thumb and forefinger, imprisoning her with the lightest of touches and making her heart, her stomach and her knees all start misbehaving. Very improperly, too. She drew in a deep shaky breath.

"I'm sorry," he said. "It's not a terrible burn, but even little burns hurt like the dickens, don't they? You need cold water. I should have done it sooner."

But she had been withholding her hand. Now she let him put her fingers beneath the cold powerful flow of the water. He let it run for a while, then shut it off.

Grabbing a clean cloth, he barely blotted her skin. A slight sting remained, but it was Owen's touch that was the far greater danger.

"This isn't the best timing, but there really isn't any good time to tell you. That phone call that Lydia took was from the mayor. He has a group coming in from Chicago to talk about an expansion of the Lambert Wood Products company to Bigsby. There's no hotel in town, at least not yet, and the closest one isn't particularly stylish. I'd agreed to house his guests a while ago, but I'd rather not expose you to too many people. Maybe it would be best if I found somewhere else for them to stay."

And here she would be causing yet another change in his life.

"Would that seem odd to the mayor?"

"Yes, but—"

"Then have them come. I can fade into the woodwork. That won't be a problem. It's what I want."

Well, it wasn't exactly all she wanted, Delfyne thought as she felt Owen's fingertips slide a bit against her skin. But what she wanted wasn't available or wise or possible in any way.

She would have to settle for playing her part and hope for the best.

CHAPTER SEVEN

OWEN'S guests had all finally arrived. Most were in their rooms getting ready for dinner, and Martin O'Casey, the mayor, was smiling with glee.

"If we can convince them that this is the perfect place to locate their business, this could be good for Bigsby," he said. "Thank you for loaning your house for this shindig, Owen. You've got the most impressive property in a hundred miles. These men and their wives like to be treated well, but I'm sure they didn't come to our town expecting anything like this," he said, gesturing around the huge, lodge-style living room with its hundreds of lights twinkling from the more than a dozen chandeliers. "Your place and Lydia's cooking will convince them that we can be just as elegant as the city."

"I don't know anyone in town who lives an elegant life, Martin," Owen said. "It's probably best not to mislead them."

Martin gave him a look that told him he was wasting his breath. "You know this business could be important."

Owen knew it was important to Martin, and Martin's father had been Owen's father's best friend.

"Are you even sure any of the people in Bigsby want a new business? The property you're talking about has any number of possible uses."

"But this one means money and jobs, and the town will want that."

Well, maybe Martin was right. Owen stuck to his ranch. He didn't really know what went on in the town half the time.

But what he knew before too much time had passed was that this event was going to be a bit different from others he'd hosted here. In the past, Lydia had hired a couple of waitresses from town to help her serve, but tonight Delfyne was doing the honors.

And things weren't going all that well.

"Miss, I'd like another one of these canapés but without so many olives. This one has too many olives," a woman said.

For a minute Owen saw a look of disapproval on Delfyne's face. "Lydia is a superb cook," she stated.

The woman looked as if a bee had just stung her. "I'm sure Lydia, whoever she may be, is adequate, but I don't like olives. Bring me one without."

For half a second Owen thought that Delfyne was going to order that the women be beheaded, but then he saw her visibly work to control her reaction. He saw now what Andreus had meant by Delfyne's temper, but to him she looked magnificent. "I'll replace it," she told the woman.

But she had barely taken a step when a man standing nearby stuck out his glass. He didn't even look her way, just expected her to take it.

Delfyne looked at him half-expectantly, then took the glass.

"You're welcome," she said, just as if he had thanked her.

"Do you have anything more bracing?" His speech was becoming slurred.

"It's extremely bad etiquette to drink too much," Delfyne said. "It's quite disrespectful of the company. Drink impairs the memory and judgment and paves the way for regretful embarrassing circumstances one cannot call back."

Uh-oh. That sounded like something right out of the *Etiquette for Royals* playbook. Andreus had once said something much the same to a fellow classmate who was making an ass of himself at a party.

Martin flashed Owen a What's-going-on-here? Do-something look.

"Excuse me? Do you have any idea who I am and how much I'm worth?" the man asked, looking down his nose at Delfyne.

All right, Owen had had enough. When tonight was over, he would never let her do this again. It was one thing to help her act out her fantasy of being an ordinary person. It was another to expose her to jerks like these. He stepped up beside the man. "The lady doesn't care how much you're worth, Mr. Baxter. Martin here, now he's the one you want to tell that stuff to."

"Yes, this must just be a misunderstanding, Baxter." Martin was practically begging. "I'm sure the girl meant well."

"She has a smart mouth on her," the woman who disliked olives said. "I'm surprised you'd allow someone so disrespectful to serve at your functions, Mr. Michaels. Here you have this beautiful place, I'd think you'd want your servers to add to the atmosphere. Part of our decision about whether to bring our business here will depend on the atmosphere. We don't want to go where we're not wanted."

Anger rose up within Owen. Had other servers at his house been treated as if they were mere appendages of the house? Had he been blind to bad behavior in his guests before?

"I assure you that Delfyne is a superlative individual with a fine character," he said. "She's much more than just a person who takes your glass and hands you food. She's an important part of our household this summer and I'd appreciate it if you'd treat her as such."

He heard Martin hiss behind him, but he ignored the warning.

Maybe this company *was* important to the region, but so was a person's dignity. A line had to be drawn somewhere.

"Owen, the town needs this deal," Martin whispered.

There was no way Delfyne or anyone else could have heard Martin, but Owen supposed the man's face would have given away his distress.

Delfyne looked at Martin and himself and gave an almost imperceptible shake of her head. Then she dipped a slight curtsy and turned toward the couple. "I beg your pardon if I appeared rude. I'm very new at this type of situation, and I'm still learning. You know much more of the proper procedures than I do, I fear. How can I make up for my inexcusable gaffe?"

Immediately the woman preened as if she had won a contest. "Well, I suppose we don't want to be the cause of a *needy* person getting into trouble. Just…go on about your business quietly, bring my husband his drink and we'll consider it forgotten."

She flung out her hand and for a moment Owen thought she was asking Delfyne to kiss it, but she was simply dismissing Delfyne. As if she were some sort of insignificant insect.

Rage boiled up within him and he started forward. Immediately he felt Martin clenching his arm. Delfyne gave him a look that screamed *Halt!* Then she headed for the kitchen.

For the rest of the evening she seemed to be an invisible shadow to everyone but him. She carried food, she took orders, she spoke only when spoken to and then only in a subservient manner.

"Thank you for allowing us to stay here. I assure you we're not all such ignorant jerks," Alex Wade, the CEO of the group said to Owen. "Still, I'm impressed that a man of your apparent stature would stand up for a server when business is at stake. You're a legend on Wall Street. The rancher who's made millions but still gets his hands dirty."

Owen turned to look at the man. "Having money doesn't

make a man blind to the needs of others. People deserve to be treated with dignity no matter their station."

"Is that a warning?"

"It might be. People around here expect fairness. Provide it and they'll go to the ends of the earth for you. Deny it and you'll fail because they'll shun you."

"Even if we offer them jobs?"

"No one around here would be allowed to starve for lack of a job."

"So you wouldn't have fired her for insubordination?"

"She's not mine to fire."

"Whose is she?"

Now Owen sat up and took notice. "Why?"

"There's something about the way she carries herself and the way she stood up to Baxter even though it was a clear risk. She intrigues me."

Owen digested that, turned it over and decided that he couldn't just let it pass.

"She's actually a guest who graciously volunteered to help out this evening. And…she's taken."

"Is she involved with you?"

Never. But he could see that this was a man who pursued what he wanted if there was half a chance he could win. "Yes," he said. Another lie.

This time Owen didn't regret the lie. Yet.

"You're not ever going to let anyone think you're my employee again. This was the worst kind of mistake and I was a jerk for putting you in the position you were in last night."

Delfyne let Owen rant on and beat up on himself for a while before she finally felt he had gotten things out of his system.

"I don't recall asking you if I could be in that position."

"I went along with it."

"To protect me."

"I don't see how it was protecting you when people were all but throwing wineglasses at you last night, demanding that you take the olives off their food and…well, all that other stuff, too. Treating you like a piece of dirt."

"It was my choice to indulge in a masquerade, not yours."

"Don't even try to tell me you enjoyed it, Delfyne."

"I wasn't going to."

"See, you hated it."

She couldn't help smiling at the chagrin in his voice.

"It was…educational."

"Learning a language is educational. The Baxters' behavior, not to mention Martin's and mine, was disgusting."

Now she frowned. "You didn't do anything!"

"Exactly."

"Well, it's not as if Martin or I would have allowed you to stop the event. And even you…well, if the town needs this company, you don't want to take food out of your people's mouths just because I suffered a few indignities last night, do you?"

"You shouldn't have to suffer *any* indignities. That wasn't a part of the deal when you came here."

"Maybe not, but I know a lot about duty, and so do you. If your people need you to bite your tongue, you do it."

A small smile transformed Owen's usually stern face into a virile expression that had surely been the downfall of many a woman. Delfyne reminded herself that she had to be careful here. She had exercised poor judgment in the past with men who were far less potent than Owen, and with men who would have at least been acceptable to her family. Money was not enough for a royal. Especially not a royal who was already promised. Duty wasn't the only important lesson she had been taught.

Honor had been hammered into her since she was two. But still…Owen was smiling and her knees were misbehaving, getting wobbly. Her heart was hammering, her breathing was…

"You needn't smile," she said, aiming for dignity and haughtiness. "Why *are* you smiling, anyway?"

"You." That smile grew, as did her consternation and susceptibility.

Delfyne forced a frown. "What about me?"

Owen reached across the table past his coffee cup and touched Delfyne's wrist right above the spot where her bracelet of bright yellow ceramic suns and turquoise beads dangled. "You try so hard to be just an everyday woman with your inexpensive bracelets and your insistence on scrubbing bathtubs and on blending in, but you can't scrub the princess out of you, Princess. She's there, always. She lives inside you."

Delfyne struggled to ignore Owen's touch. It was such a small touch, just one finger whispering across her skin. A mere breath of a touch, but she felt the effects swirling inside her and turning her to very soft butter. And his words…

She stared at his fingertip lying against her wrist. "I love my bracelets," she said and immediately regretted it. She sounded like a forlorn child. "They're one of the few things I wear just for me."

Owen uttered a low curse and without another word circled the table and hauled her up beside him. "I love these damn little bracelets, too. They drive me insane, the way they jangle and hit against your skin. I wait every day to see what each one looks like, what new part of you is revealed."

With that, he took her hand, raised it high and placed his lips against the most sensitive inner portion of her wrist, doing terrible, wonderful, exciting things to her body.

"I can hardly think when you flip your silly little bracelets. They make me crazy. *You* make me crazy."

"You're making me crazy, too," she managed to whisper. "Owen, I—" She cupped his jaw in her palm and nudged his face up so she could look into those tortured blue eyes. She knew he didn't want to do this, that he was just answering the siren's call that she had been feeling, too. She intended to say so. That's all she intended to do, but in the next instant that stupid, spontaneous part of her personality that had caused her so much trouble in her lifetime took over and she raised up on her toes and pressed her lips against his.

The minute her mouth met his, she felt a sense of finally being where she wanted to be, doing what she had been struggling against as well as an intense desire to want more, to do more.

"Kiss me," she commanded, not caring if she sounded like a princess for once.

As if she'd handed out a royal decree and he was obeying, Owen didn't hesitate. He slanted his mouth over hers. He devoured her, teased her, licked at the seam of her mouth and came inside. His warmth became her warmth, his taste became her taste. He was delicious. She was delirious.

His wide palms spanned her waist and pulled her tight against the length of his body, introducing her to a heaven she had heretofore never experienced, the just-right fit of a man who was made to please a woman.

He slid his hand lower down her spine.

"Yes. Do that," she demanded as he caressed her.

He complied and heaven grew brighter, closer…not close enough. Then his other hand cupped her breast and all sensible sensation ceased.

"This is insanity," he moaned against her lips. "I shouldn't even be touching you." But he didn't stop.

"You're right. I know you're right, but…touch me." She practically breathed the words.

She twisted and plunged her fingers into his hair. Her bracelets slapped against his head.

As if that jangling touch of ceramic against skin pulled her out of the vortex of sensation that had held her captive, Delfyne became aware of the sounds of the ranch. Lydia was right next door in the kitchen.

She didn't want what was happening here with Owen to seem cheap or tawdry or clandestine, but both of them knew it could lead nowhere. And the fact that it was even happening…would she never learn to think before she acted?

Delfyne suddenly leaned back, bleakness filling her heart. Men who knew she would never be available for the long-term had tried to take what little they could get before. The mere fact that she was off-limits had seemed to be a bonus in their eyes. And now, with Owen, she was so off-limits. They both knew that and…

"I—you were right. I can't," she said. "I'm sorry."

Owen froze. He eased back. "No. I'm sorry. I should never have touched you, Delfyne. The fact that I did…that's inexcusable under the circumstances. Andreus asked me to protect and watch over you. I stepped over the line."

Despite her own misgivings, his words appalled her. "I'm an adult, Owen. My mistakes are my own."

He opened his mouth. She placed her palm over his lips. "I don't care what task Andreus assigned you. What happens between you and me has nothing to do with Andreus."

"All right then, there are a whole lot of other reasons why I shouldn't have been kissing you."

"Agreed." She backed off and gazed up at him, her arms crossed. "But I get to take half the credit."

He frowned.

She gave him a look she had been trained to give since birth, the one that brooked no argument. She was a royal and she knew how to get her way.

To her consternation, Owen only smiled. "Nice try," he said. "But I suddenly seem to be impervious to commands. I was always stubborn."

"That's unfortunate."

"Sometimes it has been." And something dark appeared in his eyes, something she didn't want to ask him about because she knew he blamed himself for many things.

"How about a simple request, then?" she asked. "I've been kept under wraps for much of my life. I need to feel like an adult, to take credit for my own actions now and then."

He groaned. "That's the kind of request I can't refuse. I understand what you mean all too well."

She smiled. "All right. We'll watch ourselves from now on. Now, I should get back to work."

Slowly, he shook his head. "*I* have a request," he said. "Fair is fair."

Uh-oh. For some reason, that didn't sound good. But Delfyne waited.

"When you first came here, you told me that you wanted to do everything and that's why you were playing maid at last night's party. But no matter what your motivation or mine, I know that Andreus meant this summer to be a positive experience for you. Just because he didn't want to let you go off alone doesn't mean he wanted you to have a less than wonderful summer. If you're going to be in Montana, you shouldn't be kept hidden away serving food to people and having no other life. We've introduced you as a working guest on a ranch vacation. If you're a guest, you should do more than just work. You can do other things without revealing that you're a princess."

His brows were drawn together as if he wasn't quite sure where he was going next with this line of thought.

"What are you suggesting?" she asked.

"A night on the town."

"Won't that attract attention after last night?"

"Delfyne, I think you're going to attract attention no matter what."

She thought about that. "All right. What will we do?"

Owen shrugged. "There's a dinner and a dance at the Hall, a local watering hole with a view that's not to be missed. If you're going to visit Montana, you should at least witness that view. So we'll eat, we'll talk, we'll let someone else worry about the olives."

"Ah, the olives again. That really bothered you, didn't it?"

He clearly wasn't going to answer that one. "Are you going to make me beg?"

She couldn't hold back her smile. "Might be fun."

His expression hinted at exasperation. He looked like a big cat, as if he wanted to start pacing in his cage. Delfyne knew this wasn't easy for him. She'd heard that he pretty much never socialized. If he was going out on the town, he was doing it for her. And darn it, she was going to see a part of the world she hadn't yet seen.

"No begging. I'm going," she said. "I'm holding you to your word. A night on the town and a good view."

"It's a deal."

Delfyne could barely conceal her excitement at this unexpected turn of events. "What should I wear?"

He gave her a big grin. "Bracelets." And then he walked right out the door.

Well, the man was certainly insufferable. But a part of her was bubbling up inside. Owen didn't treat her like a princess. He didn't let her social standing prevent him from treating her like a normal woman.

Even if he was constantly aware of who and what she was. And so was she.

The barriers were still there and always would be.

"But not for tonight," she whispered. Tonight she would go out on the town as a regular woman on the arm of a tall, handsome cowboy who made her whole body react in a completely improper, unprincess-like manner.

CHAPTER EIGHT

OWEN hadn't been to the Hall in more months than he could remember. Maybe it had been years. Probably it had. For the past few years, ever since James had died and Faye had left, he had thrown himself into the ranch and into making money. Neither ranching nor investing were easy ventures, but the intricacies of foul weather, transient employees and the ever-changing stock market had been low-stress challenges compared to walking into the Hall with Delfyne and trying to pretend that the woman on his arm was no big deal.

She was stunningly beautiful in a plain ivory sheath with some sort of halter top that bared her shoulders. Her dark hair was pulled back, thickly braided and looped in a satiny style that emphasized the beauty of her long neck and lent credence to the school of thought that assumed every princess was born beautiful and poised and graceful. Tiny pearl teardrops were at her ears, but at her wrists, in a brazen denial of her station, the pearls on her bracelet were separated by miniature red and somewhat gaudy ceramic roses. A two-inch chain with a rose attached dangled from the catch. Owen tried not to think about removing that bracelet with his teeth.

He had to put those kinds of thoughts to rest completely now that he knew how little self-control he had around her. His job tonight was to make sure she had a wonderful evening and that no one read too much into her being here with him.

That one, he knew, might prove problematic. They were barely five feet into the room when he knew he was right. He saw Nate Hawkins nudge the man next to him and the two of them turned around and stared. At Delfyne.

And then Nate smiled. He gave Owen a "just between us men" thumbs-up sign that made Owen bristle. There was no way he wanted Nate to get the wrong idea or to indulge in public speculation that Delfyne was sharing Owen's sheets.

A slow thudding ache began to form behind Owen's eyes. He glanced down at Delfyne, who was smiling up at him. "Relax," she said, placing her hand on his arm. "*I'm* fine, in case you're worried, but *you* look very tense."

"I want this to go well for you."

"It will. Is that the gorgeous view you told me about? It was pretty from outside, but seen through windows framed in all that golden pine makes each view look like a fabulous photograph." She slipped her hand down his arm and pulled him toward one of the windows at the back of the restaurant.

"Hey, Owen!" someone called to him.

"Owen, it's good to see you. Introduce us to your lady," another someone called followed by a wild whoop.

Owen didn't stop. He called out hellos and motioned that he would introduce Delfyne later as he followed her toward the center window. Even though it was still light outside, the sun was sinking, and brilliant gold and red tints colored the earth and painted the mountaintops.

"Owen, it's so terribly beautiful. Achingly so. Why didn't Andreus ever tell me about this?"

He certainly didn't intend to mention that when her brother had been here just after college, he'd been at an age when he was most concerned with drinking and women followed by more drinking and women. And on his last trip, he'd been more concerned with helping Owen than taking in the scenery. "Maybe he wanted you to see it for yourself," he said. Which could also be the truth.

Delfyne laughed. "You're being diplomatic. If my memory serves me well, and I think it does, he more than likely spent his time here spreading the Andreus love around and sampling your wine and beer. I'm just glad that I got to see your Montana for myself. Thank you so much for bringing me here."

"Hey, Owen. What's up? What are you hiding over here for? Come on and introduce me to this gorgeous creature." The super-gruff voice came from Owen's right on the other side of Delfyne, and Owen didn't even have to look to know who it was.

"Delfyne, this is Angus Watts. He owns the ranch beyond mine. Delfyne is my guest for the summer, Angus. She's the sister of a friend."

Angus nodded thoughtfully. "Pleased to meet you," he said to Delfyne. "Owen, you should know that Molly and Martin are buzzing about Delfyne. Martin's been talking about her stirring up those people from Lambert and how their attitude ticked you off. Lots of questions flying around, including how you and Delfyne are…well, I do beg your pardon about all the gossip, Delfyne," he said, bowing slightly to her. "But Owen here is practically a hermit. Any woman who talks him out of his shell is going to cause a stir. And when that woman is a beautiful stranger who serves drinks one day and shows up in a knockout dress as the sister of an old friend the next, well…mosquitoes and the people of Bigsby will buzz. Molly even said that dress doesn't look like a knockoff, whatever that means."

Owen growled. He opened his mouth to speak, but Delfyne let out a delicious laugh that stopped him cold. "Oh, about that dinner the other night," she said with a smile. "Owen was indulging me by letting me act out a part for a few hours. It's silly, I know, but that's a job I'd never had the chance to experience, so I bullied Owen into letting me play dress-up for the night. It was an enlightening experience. I hope that I did my job well."

For half a second Angus stared like a besotted bull. Then he grinned and shook his head. "Acting? Oh, pretty lady, I'm sure you were positively wonderful," Angus said, causing Owen to stare at him sharply. Angus's eyes were locked on Delfyne, and Owen could read all the signs too clearly. Already his neighbor was enchanted with Delfyne.

"Positively wonderful," Owen drawled, and for half a second, steadfast Angus blushed red and looked embarrassed at his words.

"As a matter of fact, I was probably just okay. I think I must drive Owen nuts," she said.

Angus laughed. "Lucky Owen. I can't believe you talked him into a game of pretend. That's not like Owen at all."

Because Angus was right, and also because Owen didn't want to examine that fact too closely, he decided it was time to move to a new topic. "Thank you for warning us about the buzz, Angus," Owen told his friend. "I'll talk to Martin."

"That's good. Talk to Molly, too. You know how she likes to be queen of the town. She's going to feel hurt if she thinks you're keeping her in the dark."

"No," Delfyne said. "I'm the one who was responsible for the charade, so I'm the one who has to clear the air."

"That's not necessary," Owen said.

"Yes, it is. I don't regret getting to step outside myself, but Angus is right. I didn't even think about the ramifications of my game. And no one knows better than I how wrong and hurtful deceit and trickery can be." There was something in her voice, something pained and sad and defeated.

"What do you mean by that?"

But she shook her head. "I'm going to talk to Molly right now." She turned to go.

"Oh yeah, and you better head off Nancy," Angus told Owen. "She might need time to adjust to you being here with a new woman."

Immediately Owen felt Delfyne turn to him. "A woman upset with you? I… Am I going to cause trouble with you and your girlfriend?" she asked, and Owen could have slugged Angus.

"Nancy's not Owen's girlfriend, but she really wanted to be," Angus began before Owen held his hand up to cut him off.

"She's an old friend," Owen said. And that much was true. Whatever had or had not gone on between him and Nancy, she didn't deserve to be criticized unless the criticism was going to go both ways. She'd been a good friend to him and it wasn't her fault that he hadn't been capable of giving her all that she needed.

"Should you…go see her?" Delfyne asked. "I'll be fine on my own."

"I'll stay with Delfyne," Angus volunteered. "I'll even help her locate Martin and Molly."

Owen gave his friend a long look. "You're certainly feeling chatty and sociable tonight, aren't you?"

"That I am," Angus agreed, looking at Delfyne with more than casual interest. Well, why not? Owen had introduced Delfyne as a guest and the sister of a friend. Nothing personal about it. No reason why Angus shouldn't be interested.

Except she's a princess. She's not available to anyone, he wanted to shout. But that couldn't be spread about. It was going to be a long evening of fending off men who wanted to meet Delfyne, Owen realized as he saw Nate coming at them from the left.

Suddenly he wanted her to himself. "Talk will have to wait for later. Do you dance?" Owen asked Delfyne suddenly.

She blinked.

"Yeah, that was probably a stupid question," Owen agreed. "You dance, of course. Maybe a better question is, would you dance with me now?" He gestured toward a small dance floor at the opposite side of the room.

"I—I love to dance," she stammered, "but there's no music."

Owen didn't care. He didn't want to wait any longer. His simple plan to take Delfyne out had backfired, and now there were hurt feelings and a room full of curious onlookers. Nate was closing in, and Owen finally saw Nancy sitting at the bar. Even though she was here with a cowboy Owen didn't know, she had a look in her eye that could mean only one thing. Any minute now, she would swoop in and when she did…well, Nancy liked to ask a lot of questions. As a woman who had been lied to a lot by her ex-husband, she prided herself on being able to sense when a person was lying. Why take chances about her discovering "the rest of the story" about Delfyne?

Besides, he wasn't in the mood for any more explanations, and he had learned long ago that Nancy demanded a lot more of those close to her than he felt comfortable providing. She was a friend. At one time she had been more than a friend, but she didn't believe in boundaries or privacy or closed doors and he had far too many closed doors to please her. That hadn't stopped her from trying to pick the lock to his most private thoughts. Delfyne, with her open ways and sudden need to spill her guts for fear of hurting someone's feelings, would be a prime target for Nancy's inquisitiveness.

Moreover, he just plain old didn't want to fend off any more men ogling Delfyne and he didn't want to have to go through the motions of calling her his "guest" again. Truth to tell, he was beginning to dislike the word *guest* almost as much as he disliked the word *maid*.

"Jukebox," he explained. He took Delfyne's hand and started leading her toward the dance floor. He tossed Angus some change. "Play something slow," he said.

Not because he wanted to hold Delfyne in his arms, he told himself, but because he was pretty sure she wouldn't know any country steps, and country was pretty much all that the Hall had.

The waltzlike tune Angus picked wasn't exactly what Owen had in mind, but it made it easy to swirl Delfyne into the dance and into his arms. Just as he predicted, she was an accomplished dancer. A ballerina. A complete and true princess, born to the role.

And he was a liar of a man who was pretending she was simply his guest while wishing he could pull her closer. He was dancing with her in front of a whole crowd who knew darn well he was a man who no longer believed in tomorrow or forever. And Delfyne was a woman whose tomorrows were already claimed.

This dance had just been an impulse, an escape, but as he looked down into her eyes, her expression grew soft and warm.

"Your friends are really concerned for you," she said. "They look out for you. That says something good about you."

"They just want to meet you."

"Well, that's okay. A new face is always interesting, but this interest in how you and I are matched up is more than you think. I heard some people whispering. They said that they didn't want you to get mixed up with an interloper and outsider again. It was clear that they thought you'd been treated unfairly."

He shook his head. "They're just speculating. They don't know the whole truth about what went on with Faye. I do."

He pulled her closer and felt her nod. "Well, you may be right," she said. "Things aren't always as they seem to the outside world, are they?"

How very right she was. Right now everyone saw her as a

stranger who had some peculiar habits. They saw her as another woman who could bewitch him again and leave him raw and wounded when she finally left. As she would.

But they didn't know the half of it. And maybe neither did he.

Delfyne didn't know whether to be amused or alarmed at the way she felt both comfortable and yet excited at the feel of Owen's arms around her. She finally settled on alarm. It would be wrong and stupid for her to get used to having Owen's arms around her, to start longing for his touch. But she knew he had his reasons for keeping her on the dance floor, so when the song ended, she held out her hand.

"May I choose the next one?"

He gave her some coins with a smile that turned his eyes sexy and warm. "The music is mostly country."

"But good music is good music."

She motioned for him to follow her to the jukebox, but his presence behind her was disarming. His warmth was so close, the scent of him made her dizzy and when he spoke, he bent toward her, his lips just a whisper away from her ear, his body almost enfolding her.

Faintness threatened.

"Do you need help?" he asked her.

Oh yes, she definitely needed help. But if she asked for it, he might come closer still. She might make a total fool of herself in front of this whole crowd. Without looking, she pressed some buttons. Within seconds, loud, fast music flowed from the machine.

Delfyne didn't know the tune, but it had a driving rhythm. "Come on. I like this," she said, pulling Owen to the dance floor and starting to move to the music.

To her consternation, he didn't budge an inch.

"Owen?"

"I'm not really much of a dancer, at least not freestyle," he told her.

"Well then, we don't have to dance freestyle. You show me what to do Montana-style. Or we can just pretend this is a waltz and dance really fast. We can turn it into a polka or a jitterbug or even a rhumba." She laughed and grabbed his hand, twirling and curtsying.

He grinned and shook his head and swept her into a dance that was a combination of various styles. A few people laughed but some joined them on the dance floor and tried to imitate their moves.

When the song was over and everyone was breathing hard, Delfyne smiled up at Owen. "Excuse me," a feminine voice said. Delfyne looked over her shoulder to see the woman whose slightly angry and unhappy eyes told Delfyne that she must be Nancy. She had a man who looked to be in his mid-twenties in tow.

"Sorry for interrupting," the woman said, even though she didn't sound sorry at all. "I would have waited until Owen brought you over, but I could see he wasn't going to do that. Don't deny it," Nancy said to Owen.

He shook his head. "I wasn't going to. You were occupied and so was I. Delfyne, this is Nancy, a friend. Delfyne is—"

"I know. A house guest. You know her brother. She likes to play pretend, especially the maid game, and every man in this room is drooling over her. Do I have that right?"

"Just about," Owen conceded with a smile.

"Well, he could have introduced us earlier. I don't bite," Nancy told Delfyne.

Delfyne couldn't help liking the woman's frank ways even though Nancy had been looking daggers at her a minute ago.

Not a surprise. Every time Nancy looked at Owen, longing filled her eyes.

"You know I'm not one to make announcements," Owen chided gently. "I'm sorry if I hurt your feelings."

The air seemed to go out of Nancy. "I know." She sighed. "And you didn't hurt my feelings exactly. I just like to be the center of attention. You know that. But, Delfyne," she said, turning away from Owen and toward Delfyne. "I have to warn you. Be careful with this man. He's unfailingly honest and frank. If he tells you something is so, believe him. That was the problem with Owen and me. I told him I wasn't interested in long-term relationships. *He* said he wasn't interested in long-term relationships. But only one of us meant it."

Owen shifted uncomfortably. "Nancy, I—"

"I know. I speak my mind too much," she said, and Delfyne couldn't help but feel sorry for her. "But hey," Nancy continued. "Here's my new man, Pete. He's very cute and hot even though he's pretty much a puppy."

"Hey!" Pete objected, but already Nancy was rushing on, turning her attention back to Delfyne. "I really love that dress and the way you've made up your eyes. There's something so…I don't know…truly exotic about you. Unusual name, too. Do you have a social networking page on the Internet?"

"Excuse me?" Delfyne said, and something about the way Nancy was looking at her gave her pause. Nancy might be friendly, but she also clearly had more than a casual interest in Owen. Finding out more about the woman who was living at his house right now might be a real priority.

"You know, MySpace, Facebook…your own Web place."

"I'm sorry, no," Delfyne answered, but, of course, there was plenty of other information about her on the Internet. Photos. Articles. And her name *was* unusual.

Owen was obviously thinking the same thing. "Pete, you look really thirsty. Why don't you go buy yourself and Nancy a drink and just put it on my tab."

The young man stared at Owen in confusion for a second, but then he shrugged and veered off toward the bar.

Owen looked down at the red-haired woman he obviously had a past with, his expression grim and serious. "You've always been a very good friend, Nance. Don't change your ways now. Don't stop being a friend."

"Is that a request?" she asked.

"You can view that however you want to. The point is—and I know you already know this—I take my responsibilities seriously. Having one of my guests treated shabbily wouldn't sit well with me at all."

Nancy frowned. "Are you threatening me, Owen?"

He laughed at that. "What would I threaten you with?"

"Good point," she answered. "So, if I turned out to be my usual nosy self toward Delfyne here?"

"I would be extremely disappointed in you. No matter what our differences have been, I *have* always viewed you as a friend."

The woman uttered a swear word that Delfyne had seldom heard. "Damn you, Owen. I hate it when you use the word *disappointed*. You *know* I hate it. But, all right. I'm sure you realize that you've only intrigued me more with your *disappointment*, but I'll stay out of your business. For now at least."

She sighed and turned to Delfyne, looking anything but happy. "He really must like you a lot."

Delfyne shrugged. "It's just a big-brother kind of thing." And a lot of it was, she hated to remind herself. "He would do the same for the sister of any of his friends."

"Sounds like you know him almost as well as I do."

But she didn't, Delfyne knew. Looking up at Owen's long,

lean form and noting the affectionate smile he gave Nancy, Delfyne envied the woman her familiarity with him. She'd never had this kind of easy closeness with a man. All her experiences had been either familial or...ones she didn't want to remember or think about.

"I owe you, Nance," Owen said in that husky, gravelly voice that made Delfyne want to lean close.

Nancy laughed. "You don't owe me a thing, but I know that next week a few of my favorite charities will contact me telling me that they've received sizable donations in my name." She blew out a breath that lifted her bangs, then smiled. "You absolutely do not have to do that, Owen Michaels, but I'll accept it, anyway.

"Well, I guess I'd better go before the gossips really start wondering what we're talking about and even I won't be able to stop them. It was nice meeting you, Delfyne, whoever you are," she said softly. She took two steps toward Pete, then turned back. "Delfyne, I just have to say one more thing. Watch out for Owen, girl. He'll break your heart without meaning or wanting to. You just can't tie a man like him down, and you can't have a lot of other things a woman like you probably wants," she ended lamely with a small wave.

Owen frowned, and when Delfyne touched his sleeve she could feel the tension in his muscles. But she didn't ask any questions, even though she wanted to.

"Nancy wants babies," he said simply. "In the worst way. She should have them, too, but my friendship with her kept other men at bay. The right kind of men. Maybe Pete can finally give her what she needs."

"You feel guilty," Delfyne said softly. "Because she waited for you and expected more than you could give."

He looked at her. "Any man would feel guilty."

But Delfyne knew it wasn't so. "Did you encourage her?"

"No, of course not, but I didn't shun her, either."

"You wouldn't. Not if you were friends. Did you tell her what she could and couldn't expect?"

"I'm not a complete jerk," he said.

Delfyne couldn't help herself then. She reached up and touched his jaw. "I think you were honest with her. She said that you were. In which case…you can't be responsible for her pain. She doesn't seem like a woman who would let a man take credit for what she should take credit for."

"You're a very perceptive woman. Does that go with the package?"

She knew what he meant. "Of course. It's required of my kind."

He raised an eyebrow. "I suspect that you're one of a kind."

Delfyne's heart swelled. She was almost grateful that Angus and some more of Owen's friends appeared at that time and started talking to him. She needed a moment to compose herself, to try to remember who and what she was and who and what *he* was. And that there was no common ground. Not really.

But she had no time to dwell on that. Nancy's visit seemed to have broken the ice, and for the next hour people came up and introduced themselves. They talked business with Owen, and some of them appeared to be begging monetary favors. He asked them questions about their feelings regarding the wood products company, whether it was something they wanted or needed and how he could help them. And all of them looked at Delfyne with unrepentant curiosity.

She explained her charade to Molly and Martin, offering her apologies and telling Molly as much of the truth about her situation as she could. As she and Molly bonded on the dance floor, the easy way the woman accepted her explanation nearly brought tears to Delfyne's eyes. She hoped Molly wouldn't be hurt if the whole truth ever came out.

Some of the men asked Delfyne to dance, and at one point, she and Molly corralled everyone and got a conga line going, which made Owen roll his eyes. Still, as if Owen and Nancy had sworn them to secrecy, no one delved too deeply into the personal beyond mentioning Delfyne's maid charade.

"Heck that must have been kind of fun. Sort of like Halloween in the off season," one woman said.

"Exactly," Delfyne exclaimed and barely stopped herself from explaining that she had never actually experienced an American Halloween. That would only have elicited questions she couldn't answer without saying too much.

"I love playing dress-up," another woman cut in. "Even though some people think it's rather juvenile. I know. Let's have a costume party next Halloween. Maybe we could even get Owen to wear something yummy. Like a gladiator costume or something. I'll bet he looks real good without his shirt on."

"Hmm, there's a thought," Delfyne said with a smile, turning around to look for him and finding him not three feet away. She reached out and tugged on his arm, snagging his attention. "*Do* you look good without your shirt on?"

Owen blinked, then gave her a simmering look that curled her toes and sent heat spiraling through her body, but told her she was treading on thin ice. "I don't know what all of you have been talking about, but don't encourage her," he told the women, who simply laughed.

"Let's plan something," they told her.

"That would be fun," Delfyne agreed as she bade her goodnights. But of course, there was no point in planning anything. She would be gone long before October. Everything here—life, the ranch and Owen—would go on without her. It would be as if she'd never been here at all.

Now was the time to make memories. It was the *only* time.

CHAPTER NINE

OWEN breathed a sigh of relief when he finally got Delfyne outside. Despite the fact that his friends had been friendly and polite, he knew that a lot of them were more than curious about Delfyne.

Even if she was dying to know every gritty detail there was to know about Delfyne, Nancy would stand by her word and corral her curiosity, at least until Delfyne's visit was over. He couldn't be so sure about other people, and much as he'd like to threaten to split some heads he couldn't do that. It would only intrigue people more.

"I probably shouldn't have brought you out tonight," he told her. "I bet at least half a dozen people are already looking you up on Google."

She turned to face him. "I know, but we didn't tell anyone anything other than my first name, and this night was so worth the risk of exposure. I had fun."

"I can't believe you got Doug Spears to pretend he was a karaoke singer. He's going to wake up in the morning totally red-faced once the beer wears off."

She punched him. "He is not. He was good!"

Owen laughed. "He was, but that you actually talked him into it…Doug is about the shyest man I know. I can half see why Andreus was so worried about you."

Delfyne was suddenly quiet. She looked away.

"That wasn't a complaint or a criticism," he said gently.

"I know, but—" She sighed. "Sometimes, Andreus is right. I do go too far at times. I confused Molly and probably hurt her feelings and I really have to work on curbing my tendency to jump in without thinking. In my world, being watchful and careful is part of life. It's necessary."

And because she knew her world and its requirements, he had to assume she might be right. He hated to think that life would judge her unfairly. For half a moment he thought of the prince she was to marry and hoped the guy wouldn't criticize her or try to tame her spirit too much. Anger at the thought boiled up in Owen, but he didn't have the right to feel that way, to feel any way at all where she was concerned. With difficulty, he fought his anger and set it aside.

But on the ride home both of them were quiet.

The next day brought something unexpected: visitors. Lots and lots of visitors.

Owen had left so early that he hadn't had a chance to see Delfyne, and, wanting to make sure she wasn't suffering buyer's remorse about her night on the town, went up to the house to check on her. He was halfway through the door when a sound he'd avoided for a long time met his ears. A baby was laughing. In his house.

He went cold. Then hot. Then cold again. Crushing pain hit him full in the chest. He staggered a bit as he walked through the kitchen, then caught himself. In the living room he found Delfyne sitting next to a woman he didn't know. The woman was holding a child about a year old, older than James had been but still with that chubby wide-eyed innocence about him.

Owen felt faint. He fought the light-headedness. The little boy was studying him intently.

"Buh," the boy said.

Owen closed his eyes. James's tiny face, wreathed in smiles, swam in his memory. His boy had never lived to talk.

"Owen?" Delfyne's worried voice broke in and he turned to see her and the oblivious young mother studying him.

The little boy squealed in delight again and bucked on his mother's lap.

Owen tried to control his urge to flinch. Obviously not successfully. "I'm afraid when he takes a liking to something or someone he's not old enough yet to realize how loud he is," the mother explained.

Shaking his head, Owen held out his hand. "He's fine," he managed to say in a voice that was a bit lower and thicker and far more ragged than usual.

"Cute little guy, isn't he?" he said, faking a smile for the mother and Delfyne's sake.

"This is Charley. He's adorable," Delfyne agreed. She introduced him to Janet, who was new in town and had met Delfyne last night. "I thought you were working," she admonished, but what she meant, he knew, was *I thought it would be okay to have this woman and baby over while you were gone.*

"I was. I am," he said. "I just forgot something in my room. Please, go on with your visit," he said, though he could see that Delfyne wanted to say more.

But what could she say in front of the woman? He knew she wouldn't do anything to make the young mother uncomfortable and he would never want her to. So, pasting on the biggest, fakest smile he could muster, he winked at the child, nodded to the mother and swiftly went to his room.

Once there he took deep long breaths. He fought against memories of the past and tried not to think about the stricken look in Delfyne's pretty eyes. He hated that he had made her feel that she had done something wrong or that he had caused her even one second of worry.

Grabbing up the first thing at hand, he quickly marched back downstairs, held up the object, which turned out to be a comb. Then he smiled brilliantly, exchanged thirty seconds of pleasantries with Delfyne's guest and went back out the door to his truck. There was plenty of work to keep him busy, and he stayed away as long as he could.

When he finally pulled back into the yard, Delfyne came out to meet him.

"Owen, I—"

He held up one hand to stop her. "Don't even think about saying you're sorry. Babies are a fact of life."

"But not in your house, they're not."

"I can't hide from every child in the world."

But he did his best. She'd probably guessed that, but he didn't want her beating up on herself for his flaws. Andreus had sent her here because of what her brother felt were *her* flaws. She'd been hidden away because of that. She certainly didn't need to take on more restrictions.

He came toward her and took her hands. "Delfyne, you met a friend, someone who liked you. She came to visit you. You invited her in. Do you think I would have expected you to ask her to take her baby home?"

She shook her head, a wistful, worried look in her eyes. He thought she'd say no and that would be the end of that.

"Tell me more about your past, about what makes you… you," she said. Of course, she wasn't a woman who would do the easy thing and ignore his thorny past the way everyone else did.

He sat down on the porch and drew her down with him. "There's not much to tell. This ranch has been in my family for four generations. It's a demanding life. At least, if you're really going to ranch and not hire someone else to do the work it is."

"You wouldn't hire someone, would you?"

He shrugged. "If I did, I'd just be playing a game."

"The gentleman rancher," she said with a soft smile.

"Yes. Anyway, my father went away on a trip and brought my mother back here, where she proceeded to wilt and disappear, she said. After I was born, she got worse. Before that she had been unhappy, feeling tied to the ranch and my father, but having a child was even worse. It meant beginning a dynasty, really becoming glued to the lifestyle. It was as if she hadn't really committed herself to my father, but once I came along she knew she had to do that or leave. She chose to leave. And he became an angry, bitter man. This ranch and I became his world."

"I would think you would hate it."

"You would, wouldn't you? But it was never that way. I've always felt as if part of my soul goes missing when I leave here. I went away to college, but part of me was here. I traveled, I made money elsewhere, but this was where I found my greatest satisfaction. And like my father, I found my bride and brought her back here."

"She hated it, too?"

"Not right away. Part of her even liked it, but it wasn't enough. She was…a collector of sorts and she liked to have things that were outside the norm. Where she came from a rancher was an oddity, but once she'd collected a rancher, she needed to move on to the next thing, to have more. To her credit, she tried to hide her unhappiness. She felt she'd made a pact and she needed to be a grown-up and stick to it even if she grew more weary of the life every day. She missed the city. She missed being at the center of fun, the lights and the noise. But she stayed. Until James died. And then we both discovered that he was the only glue holding us together."

"So she left you and now you stay here alone and avoid babies."

She sounded so sad that he couldn't hold back a laugh. "I'm not a sad man, Delfyne. I like my life. It's full enough."

"But you won't marry."

"It's doubtful. Every woman I meet gets hurt by my reticence to commit. You saw that with Nancy. They all seem to feel I'm not giving my all. And I suppose I'm not."

"*I* suppose you have reason. Why should you give your heart when it's been thrown back at you by women who held it in their keeping? And not wanting to have another child, of course you wouldn't make promises you didn't intend to keep when you'd already been on the wrong end of a broken promise yourself. But I wish I could make things right for you, give you something."

He chuckled and shook his head. "Ah, I see. Now you're being the benevolent lady, bestowing her gifts upon the poor hapless knight who came calling."

She gave him a mock incredulous look. "Well, you certainly don't look hapless, much less like a knight right now. You've torn your shirt," she said, laying her palm over the ripped section just above his heart. Her skin was warm.

And suddenly the world shifted. The very air seemed to change. Owen's heart thudded crazily as if a woman had never touched him before.

"And…" She licked her lips nervously. "And a knight would never sit side by side with…with his…"

"Shh, don't say it. Someone might hear," he whispered, leaning near. And then his lips found the sensitive skin beneath her ear.

She shivered.

"Would a knight do that?" he wondered.

"I—I don't think so," she began.

"Then maybe this." He nuzzled his way farther down her neck. She tilted her head to give him better access, and heat flared within him. Slipping his arms around her, he kissed her, he touched her, he slid his palms up her torso, his thumbs resting beneath her breasts.

"Don't worry about me, Delfyne," he urged, his mouth dancing over her skin. "Please. Don't try to make me feel better, don't make me into something more or better than I am. I'm a rancher, simply a rancher. The fact that I have more money than most doesn't make me any different. And the fact that I'm kissing you now when I know that there's no future in it for either of us, no wisdom in it at all, means I'm worse than most. Don't trust me, ever. I don't trust myself."

With that, he let her go. He rested his forehead against hers for a minute and listened to the sound of their deep, uneven breathing.

"Go inside now," he said in a voice that betrayed the fact that letting her go was too damn difficult to enable him to speak clearly.

"I wasn't teasing you," she said. "I—that is, I was. We were playing, but I didn't mean my pretense to cause you regret."

He smiled against her forehead. "If you think I regret touching you, you're dead wrong, Delfyne. It's what I'm not going to do that I regret."

She looked at him and kissed the corner of his mouth. "I wouldn't have stopped you."

He groaned. "Could you please not tell me that? Or could you at least try a lie?"

She smiled against his skin. "All right. I wish you hadn't kissed me, and actually a part of that isn't a lie. Because once I leave here, I can't ever look back and wonder what would have happened next. Sometimes it's best not to know desire at all, I think."

"Delfyne…" he said on a groan. "All right, I am sorry."

"Don't be. That part, the touching, was wonderful, but also not wise. Because from here on out, this moment of weakness and desire will always be between us."

And with that she got up and went inside.

She was right, he thought. More right than she knew. Long after she had forgotten her brief moments on the porch of a ranch with a man she should never have met, he would be remembering the taste of her.

There was an edginess between Owen and herself for the next few days, Delfyne couldn't help noticing. She knew he was blaming himself, but really she was the one who had started the teasing. She had a distinct feeling that Owen didn't get teased very often.

She had pushed him too far. As she always did.

Now she wanted to make up in some small way, so she set to work on learning to make that cake. Lydia had told her that double fudge surprise was Owen's favorite, and Delfyne was determined to make him the lightest, fluffiest, most delicious cake he had ever tasted. Better than Lydia's.

"Or maybe almost as good as Lydia's," Delfyne whispered out loud as she mixed ingredients. She had better get it right. Lydia had run into town with Nicholas—who'd taken to ranch duty so well, Delfyne wondered if he'd rather be a cowboy than a bodyguard—to pick up a replacement part for her vacuum cleaner. There was no one to consult if Delfyne made a baking mistake.

In fact, she was concentrating so hard that she almost didn't hear the knock at the door, but finally it snagged her attention just as the person started to bang harder. "Lydia, damn it, open up. I'm frying my butt off out here."

"I'm on my way," Delfyne said. "Just let me wipe my hands." She pulled up a piece of her apron and did just that as she hurried to the door.

Standing on the kitchen stoop was a big, grizzled man, and he looked miffed. "Took you long enough. I was ready to come through the window," he said.

"I'm sorry. I didn't hear you. Come in," she said. "Are you looking for Lydia? Or Owen?" She moved into the house to get the two-way radio.

But when she turned around, the man had moved up right behind her. He was staring at her intently. "I'm here to see Owen. We've got business, but now that I'm out of the hot sun, there's no need to hurry," he said. "Who are you? Anyone else here?"

Something in his voice and his words didn't sound or feel right. Definitely the way he was staring at her was wrong. There was something too fierce and wrong about his interest. He glanced to the side as if looking out the window, but Delfyne knew that no one was there.

Panic began to rise within her as she realized that she had let down her guard and let this stranger into the house. Used to her bodyguards screening her contacts, she had simply assumed she was safe and plunged ahead without thinking. But people came through here all the time. Lydia let them in. She talked to them. So did Owen. Friends, neighbors, business people stopped by. Those people weren't strangers, and obviously this man wasn't either.

Taking a deep, enervating breath, she tried to remember who she was and how to command respect and maintain a distance. "Who are *you*?" she countered, but her voice came out too shaky.

He smiled slyly, and right away she hated that smile. "You don't have to worry about me. Owen knows me. I live in the next county. Owen mentioned that he had a likely stallion to service my best mare. I came to look."

But as he said the words, he reached out to touch.

"Don't!" Delfyne said, sliding back and away.

"Hey, don't be so skittish and fussy. I'm not going to hurt you," the man said, continuing his advance. "You have chocolate on your cheek. I'm going to rub it off." But his voice was thick and his hand was unsteady and his eyes—

"I'll wipe it off later," she said, taking a step back.

"Oh, I don't mind helping at all." His thick fingers made contact with her skin.

"Do *not* touch me!" she ordered in her best princess voice, through teeth that chattered. And she ducked away and headed for the front door, her knees shaking.

The door flew open in front of her and Owen stepped inside.

His eyes blazed as he looked past her to the man. "Dekins, get out of my house," he said.

"Owen, I wasn't doing a thing. I don't know why the stupid woman was screeching like that. You know me. You know why I'm here. And she asked me to help her."

Owen didn't even look at Delfyne for verification or denial. "Frankly, I don't care what she did or didn't do. You're not to touch her. Now, get out."

The man started forward. "Owen, you've known me for years. I didn't do a thing wrong. She let me in. She's—"

He never finished the sentence. Owen's fist smashed into his face and the man reeled backward, struggling to stay on his feet.

"Not another word," Owen told him. "Any business you and I had is concluded. For good," he said. "Don't come back on my land again."

The man cast Delfyne and Owen a look of hatred, but he left the house, climbed in his truck and roared away, his tires spinning and spitting gravel.

When he was gone, Delfyne dared to look at Owen. He was breathing hard. His eyes were dark with anger.

"Did he hurt you?"

She swallowed hard.

"Delfyne?"

"No." She shook her head vehemently. "He just scared me. He touched my cheek and he looked at me as if he was going to—"

Owen reached out and pulled her to him. He crushed her against him. "I never did like him much. Good riddance. The man is total dirt."

Delfyne closed her eyes and breathed in the warm male scent of Owen. She felt safe against his hard body. But…

Pulling back, she looked up into his eyes. "I *am* partly at fault. I *did* let him in. That was very stupid of me. And so…typical. Andreus and my family are right about me. I'm too unpredictable and spontaneous. I act first and think later. This was as much my fault as that man's."

"Like hell it was. There's never an excuse for a man trying to touch an unwilling woman."

"But maybe by letting him in the door, I was inviting something I never meant to. That is…sometimes things happen that way and…"

Memories of other mistakes she'd made crept in. Delfyne closed her eyes.

The next thing she knew Owen was lifting her into his arms. He carried her to the nearest sofa and sat down with her, holding her.

"'Sometimes things happen that way'?" he said. His voice was icy. "What on earth has someone done to you, Delfyne?"

She leaned against him, trying to breathe, to think, to *not* think. "I don't want to tell you. I don't want to tell anyone. Ever."

"Yeah, like that's going to stop me from asking. Now that I know that someone has hurt you, I… Tell me now."

"Once you know, you'll respect me less than you already do."

"You say that as if I don't respect you."

Her laugh was brittle. "My brother pawned me off on you because I couldn't be trusted to handle myself. How could you respect someone like that?"

She sat up taller and gazed into those blue eyes.

He placed his hands on her forearms and pulled her within a

breath of his lips. "You don't have a clue what I think about you. Frankly, neither do I, because I spend a lot of time trying to avoid thinking about you, but when I do allow myself a few thoughts, I can guarantee that none of them have to do with disrespect."

They stared at each other for five full seconds. She swallowed and struggled to keep breathing, to keep from leaning closer to him.

"So tell me, Princess, what happened to you?"

She shook her head. She hesitated. Finally, she just waded in. "I grew up much the way I am now. Always expecting the best, not stopping to think that anything bad could happen to me, rushing in to do whatever I wanted to do. And…I think a part of me really believed in the princess fairy-tale story. I was a romantic. Even though I knew my parents were brokering a marriage for me with another suitable royal, a part of me believed that that was unimportant. Irrelevant. That it could be ignored or prevented. Love was possible."

"I see you're talking in the past tense. What changed your mind?"

She flung out one hand. "I was seventeen. Some other royals were visiting, and one of them was an eighteen-year-old boy. We flirted, we swam, we danced, eventually we kissed. I fell hard. Head over heels, as they say. I was ecstatic, transformed. Now my life would change. I imagined that we would talk on the phone, write, visit. We'd convince our parents of the need to tear up my marriage contract and his. But the night before he left, he tried to…do more than I was ready for, and I told him that I wanted to wait until we knew each other better."

She paused and began fidgeting with the buttons on Owen's shirt. "I take it that he disagreed?" His hands tightened on her.

"He laughed at me. He told me that we weren't going to know each other better. I was a weekend fling. Knowing that I was off-limits and that I couldn't possibly demand more, he'd assumed

"You're not taking the blame because some royal jerk couldn't keep his pants on. Andreus should know. Your family should know, and the prince should never be allowed near you again."

"It's too late now. I didn't say anything then, and now I can't. And I'm not taking the blame. I know I didn't invite his advances in any way, and I'm sure I should have said something right then, but…he's married now and he has a baby. The princess is a good woman who keeps him on a short leash, and I don't want to cause a scandal because of something that happened two years ago when in the end nothing happened. I'm pretty sure he was drunk. I've heard nothing that has led me to believe that any other girls have been in danger. I think that's part of why I tend to believe my own exuberance might have been misunderstood. My family thinks I'm uncontrollable, and to some extent they're right."

"There's *nothing* wrong with you."

"Owen, I let a total stranger into the house a few minutes ago," she said, rising to stand beside him, and to her surprise she was calmer now. Something about Owen's presence and his touch, his championing of her soothed her.

"He wasn't a stranger. He's been here many times."

"He was a stranger to me. In most books that makes me a woman too stupid to exist."

"You're not even slightly stupid. Andreus once complained that you were a far better student than he was."

"Well, I'm not stupid, no, but I *am* impulsive and you can't deny that. It's a despicable trait, it makes me read people wrong and…Owen, I just thought of something. That man—he's probably going to bring a lawsuit against you for hitting him. That's so unfair, but don't worry. My bodyguards can dissuade him. They're very good at that kind of thing, you know."

For the first time during this entire exchange Owen laughed.

"What?" she asked.

"Okay, you *are* impulsive," he agreed. "And given that last statement, maybe even a little bloodthirsty, but you're absolutely not to blame because men have behaved badly with you. And I don't want you worrying about a lawsuit. If it comes to that, I can afford the best lawyers around. And I can afford to pay any damages the jackass might win."

She looked up at him, stricken. "The paparazzi are going to love this so much."

"That's true. I completely forgot about them. Well, that's not going to be an issue. I'll handle this."

"Owen, really. I so do not want you to have to pay him money to keep him quiet. Even if you can afford it. That's just not right when you were trying to do a good thing for me."

She couldn't keep the sadness from her voice, and he gently tipped her face up to his.

"Andreus shouldn't have asked you to invite me," she said. "Look at that. You've bruised your poor hand and now you're shelling out money to keep my name out of the news and…"

"And…shh," he said. He kissed her, quickly, then put her aside.

"For the record, no matter how attracted to you I am, I would never try to talk you into doing something you didn't want to do," he said.

She looked up at him, indignant. "I know that. You think I don't know that?"

He stuck his thumbs in the back of his jeans' pockets and blew out a breath. "What I know is that I've gone crazy kissing you several times, and we both know that's leading nowhere. And I don't want to be another of those guys trying to seduce you. I like you and respect you too much to do that."

"Do you think I don't know that, too?"

"You've already told me you have bad judgment where men are concerned."

She crossed her arms. "I did not say that. I said that once, *when I was seventeen*, I misread a boy. After that, I had several instances where men just happened to think that my situation and the fact that I tend to be a bit too vivacious and spontaneous made them think I would be easy to seduce. You, I recall, didn't like this setup from the start. I don't think you feel that anything about my visit is easy, and rightfully so given all the upheaval, lies and bruised hands you've suffered since I arrived. Today…that man was here to do business with you, so now I've even cost you a business deal."

Owen smiled a sad smile, raised one finger and brushed her nose lightly with his fingertip. He bent and kissed her so softly, she barely felt it. "You're right. I like you too much, Delfyne, but there's nothing about you that's easy," he agreed. Then he went to the door. "But if anyone—and I mean *anyone*—gives you any trouble or scares you in any way, ever again, I want you to scream at the top of your lungs. Call my name. Say anything, and I'm there, Princess. No one is going to take you lightly or misread you while you're here with me."

CHAPTER TEN

OWEN spent the next few days trying both to stay away from Delfyne and to stay near enough to be there if she needed him. He thought he'd succeeded until Delfyne came marching out to where he was changing the oil on one of the trucks.

"*Don't* do what you're doing," she said, bending over sideways trying to see him beneath the truck.

Owen, doing a task he had done hundreds of times, had been trying his hardest not to let his thoughts dwell on Delfyne, so when she suddenly appeared out of nowhere, he half thought he'd conjured her up. Rising up too suddenly, he rammed his forehead into the underbelly of the truck and let forth a streak of words he never would have ordinarily uttered in the presence of a princess.

"Oh, Owen," she said in some distress. "I'm so sorry. I guess I should have whispered."

Despite his pain, he couldn't help laughing as he got to his feet. "I don't think a breathy whisper from an intriguing woman would have made a difference, Delfyne. It probably would have played right into my fantasy."

"Oh." She looked taken aback. "A fantasy. I see. With me."

"Don't worry. I don't intend to act on it."

"Of course not. You made that very clear the other day." For some reason she seemed a bit miffed. Owen didn't even want to think about that. "That's very good of you."

Good had nothing to do with it. He couldn't keep his mind off her. If he even allowed himself to indulge his wayward thoughts, nothing positive would come of that.

"What was it you wanted me to stop doing?" he asked. "You said—"

For a moment she looked flustered. Then she crossed her arms again in that cute regal way she had. "Yes, I meant Theron and Nicholas. Stop siccing them on me. They're unhappy having their regular work taken away from them."

"I was under the impression that they had been hired to watch over you."

"Yes, but they're under my orders and I really don't need them. I'm perfectly safe. No more opening door to strangers. I completely understand that now. So, you can let the men get back to their tasks. There's no need to worry."

Of course, that only made him worry more. It was when Delfyne was at her least concerned that she failed to be on her guard.

He hesitated.

"I know what you're thinking," she said, "but I'm not without tools. When Lydia heard what happened she gave me a whistle and some pepper spray and she made me watch her self-defense tapes. I practiced on Theron and now I can take a man down if I have to. Lydia has quizzed me."

"Take a man down in hand-to-hand combat? Hmm, remind me to give Lydia a raise. She's a saint." For some reason his voice came out a bit raspy.

"She thinks of you as a son. She told me that I had to be smart not only so I wouldn't get hurt, but so you wouldn't worry. And because ranch women are strong and tough and independent."

"And a bonus. I'm giving her a bonus."

"She raised you, didn't she?"

"Like a mother. Better than a mother."

Delfyne's smile was brilliant. "I'm glad. And I'm happy that you have someone here who cares about you that much. Well, I'd better get back to my cake. And…Lydia is teaching me to use the other stove. I've graduated." She looked so thrilled and her smile was so bright that Owen's heart hurt.

"If Lydia thinks you're ready, then you are."

She nodded. "I know. It's silly to get excited over something so trivial, but I am. And, Owen?"

He waited.

"I'm ready for something else, too."

For a second, desire engulfed him and the blood pounded in his ears. Then he shook his head. Of course, she wasn't talking about that.

"My time here is moving along. Most of the people around here have met me, and they've accepted me, even welcomed me. I don't want to hide away anymore. I want to know more about the ranch. The things outside the house. It's time. I won't have this kind of opportunity again in my lifetime."

"You could always visit the ranch again. Would anyone really say no to a princess?"

"No, it wouldn't be the same at all. Once I leave here, my life will be very public again. My privacy will be gone, and every event in my life will *be* an event, not a simple everyday occurrence. If I'm to experience your world in any real sense, it has to be now."

"I don't know who ever told you that you weren't a wise woman, but they were very wrong."

She laughed. "No one ever said I wasn't wise. Just headstrong. The two aren't always mutually exclusive. But you haven't responded to my request."

"I'll see what I can arrange."

"I want it to be you who shows me. Only you."

With difficulty he held his stance and didn't move toward her. If ever there was a woman he shouldn't touch or have any illusions about regarding the future, it was this one. Once she was gone, she was gone. This time, unlike his experiences with his mother and his wife, hope had never existed. There hadn't been any possibilities.

"I wouldn't trust you to anyone else," he said.

"I just—I know I'll be safe with you." Which just about buckled his knees. She intended to trust him. He had to merit that trust.

"Let me clear my calendar and make sure that Ennis and Len and Morgan have everything under control. Then I'll be free to be your tour guide. I'll be at your service."

She shook her head. "Not at my service. Just with me. My guide but my friend. The only male friend I've ever really known."

The burden grew heavier. The honor grew greater. Owen felt warmth growing within him. "I haven't had many female friends, either. Not like you mean."

"You've had Nancy. You'll still have Nancy when I'm gone. I'll never have a man for a friend again. It's the kind of thing that would be talked about even if it were perfectly innocent. I want and need this time with you."

She was wrong about Nancy. That relationship was nothing like this, but he knew what she meant. "Then you'll have this time, and I'll try to make it as special as I can. I'll be your friend."

He had no idea how he was going to manage this without feeling too much or wanting too much, but…she was placing her trust in him. She was giving him a gift he'd never been given before. If it took every ounce of his self-control, he intended to manage this.

And heaven help him if he slipped up and touched her.

* * *

Okay, she had gone and done it, Delfyne thought the next day. She had used the *f*-word and not the bad one, either, but it had all been such a lie. That is, of course she valued Owen's friendship. This was the man who had opened up his house and his life to her even though he hadn't wanted to. He had agreed to hide her from the reporters and had danced with her to protect her. He'd hit someone for her. And he was good to his employees. He was a hands-on employer even though he had the money to hire more people to do all the work for him.

The problem was that she wasn't sure she could think of him as just a friend. The man made her feel as if Ping-Pong balls were bouncing around inside her every time he simply looked at her.

"Oh well, I asked for this, and darn it, I want it. Wish me luck, Timbelina," she said, picking up the taffy-colored cat that had been hanging around the house more often lately.

"Timbelina?" Owen's voice came from behind her, and there they were again. Those darn Ping-Pong balls.

"I thought she was a boy at first and I was calling her Tim, so when I found out I was not just wrong but that she was pregnant, well, she's small for a cat, so…Tim became Thumbelina became Timbelina. See?"

He chuckled "I see that your cat wants to roam." He was right. Timbelina was struggling, probably because Owen's presence was doing weird things to Delfyne's insides, making her squeeze the cat just a bit too tightly.

"I'm very sorry," she said to the cat, who looked at her with what could only be called pity. Whether the look was because Delfyne didn't know how to hold a cat or because the animal sensed Delfyne's susceptibility to Owen wasn't clear.

"Are you…ready for a tour?" he asked.

"I think so." She held out her arms so that he could see that she was dressed in jeans, a shirt that would protect her arms, a

CHAPTER ELEVEN

DELFYNE felt like an idiot for admitting her foolish fears to Owen of all people. She'd ridden horses after that fall even though she was nervous every time she was up so high off the ground. But Owen was so protective of her that she should have known her admission would make him feel guilty.

Amazingly enough, she did feel safe riding this sweet horse he had chosen for her with him by her side. And she felt something else, too. Attraction. Heat. Longing. He was so masculine, so tall in the saddle, so utterly right for this land. How could any woman not want to get close to him? How could any woman who had been kissed by him not think about wanting his hands and his mouth on her?

Delfyne lurched and Kitty shied, then relaxed back into her gentle walk.

Immediately Owen turned to her. She held up her hand. "I'm fine," she assured him. But she had better stop letting her mind wander down forbidden paths.

"Tell me about what we're seeing," she urged.

He shrugged, and even that was sexy. "The Second Chance is large by Montana ranch standards, so we're just going to hit a few places today. I'll show you what some of the men are doing. I have to warn you though, it's not nearly as exciting as what you read in books or see in the movies."

"I know, but still…show me. Tell me."

"I will. It's a year-round job, seven days a week. A lot of it is dirty—beyond dirty. There are smells and bad weather and un-cooperative animals."

She laughed.

"What?" he asked.

"It sounds as if you hate it, and I know that's not true," she said.

"It's right for me, but most people…a few weeks of ranching would be enough for a lifetime. Cows spend a whole heck of a lot of their time eating, and there are significant parts of the year when there's no grass available and we have to supply them with food. It's heavy, never-ending work muscling bales of hay. In the winter the weather is sometimes dangerously cold, but the job still has to be done every day, and cutting and baling hay to maintain that supply is a major summer task. Even when there's grass available for them in the summer and they can be turned out to pasture, we have to make sure that they don't have access to any poisonous weeds, so we have to eliminate those." He went on to explain briefly about keeping the equipment in good shape, calving and branding and moving cows from pasture to pasture and doing all that was involved to keep the animals healthy.

"But you do it all."

"It's my job, same as visiting hospitals and so on is yours," he said.

"And you love it," she prompted.

Owen laughed. "You sound pretty sure about that."

"Of course. You're here, aren't you?"

He sobered. "I'll always be here. That's the way it is." Because he had to stay. His heart was here. His child was buried here.

She obviously knew what he was talking about because she

sidled Kitty over and touched his arm, not even thinking about the horses. "I hope you're not apologizing for being who you are."

"Stubborn?" he asked, trying to bring a teasing tone to the conversation.

She laughed, but she didn't contradict him.

He took her to where Nicholas was baling hay and where Theron was cleaning out an irrigation ditch. He pointed out a distant pasture where some of the men were moving cows using dirt bikes. Soon Owen was leading her past a pretty little creek with a surprisingly old and tiny house sitting next to it.

"What a lovely area for a house. Does someone live here?" she asked.

Owen dismounted and came over, helping her from her horse. She slid down his body, and for a moment they stared at each other, his hands on her as her heart slammed around inside her chest. She wanted nothing more than to lean forward and connect with him and because she wanted him so badly, this man she couldn't have, she had to break the spell that was threatening to overtake her. *One kiss, just one kiss*, she thought.

It won't be enough, was her next thought. *Not nearly.*

With a Herculean effort she placed her hands on his shoulders and pushed back. He lowered her to the ground.

"No one has lived here for a long, long time," he told her. "This was the original homestead. Jenny Milner came here with her husband and they had three children together. When he was gored by a bull and died, she tried to go on alone but with three children under age five it was very difficult and they were barely surviving. Then one day a young soldier who was headed west after the Civil War passed by and saw her. She was five years older than him, but he didn't care. Three weeks later he asked to marry her despite the fact that she told him that she would never stop loving her husband. He told her that he still wanted her and he was willing to marry her and raise her children as his own as long as they could build a new house so that her husband wouldn't be there between them all the time. She could visit the old house as often as she liked."

"That's sad," Delfyne said.

"It was part of the harsh realities of the west. Survival was very difficult. And in the end, she fell in love with him anyway. But she still came here every year and planted flowers on her husband's grave. Her new husband put up a headstone to replace the wooden cross that was disintegrating."

"Was that soldier one of your relatives?"

"He was the one who named the ranch. She was his second chance after losing everything in the war, and he was hers."

"You have deep roots here," she said. "This is your history."

"This is my everything," he agreed.

She knew that he didn't lie. This ranch was like a loved one to Owen. He was married to the Second Chance, committed totally and forever. How could his wife not have realized that?

But maybe she had. Maybe Faye couldn't stand knowing that Owen would always love the Second Chance best. And maybe she had been a fool to ask for more.

"We'd better go back," he said. "You have an appointment."

"Yes. I need to be there. Thank you for bringing me out here. Your ranch is beautiful, Owen, what I've seen of it. It must have been wonderful back in the days when people slept out under the stars. I guess they don't do that anymore. Before I leave I would like to see more of it."

"More?"

"Everything."

He smiled at her. "You use that word a lot."

"I guess I do. I want a lot out of life."

He came closer. "You should have a lot. You should

have…everything. You constantly amaze me. Why would a woman like you want to sleep outside when you can sleep anywhere you like?"

Except with him, she reasoned. She couldn't sleep with him.

"I'm a romantic, I guess," she said. "It would be romantic."

"You'd hate it," he said with a grimace. "Have you ever slept outside?"

"No, but I've imagined it."

"Imaginations lie. There are bugs. No soft mattresses, no plumbing. A lot of people can't deal with that."

She knew he was thinking of Faye, imagining what his mother and his wife had thought their married lives would be like and what reality had turned out to be. And she knew she couldn't win this argument. "But I don't lie about important things," she said, "and I told Lydia I'd be back in time to make dinner. That's important, so we need to get back. I'll need time to curry the horse first."

He helped her back on her horse and they rode home in silence.

"You don't have to do this," he said when she asked him to show her what to do with Kitty. "You have things to do and horses aren't your favorite animals."

"Kitty is my new favorite creature next to Timbelina. She was very sweet with me, not like that big dark beast my trainer insisted that I ride."

So Owen showed her how to brush Kitty. He placed his hand over hers on the curry comb and they made circles on the horse's coat until Delfyne didn't think she could stand his touch anymore.

"You can go," Owen finally told her through gritted teeth.

"You can't run me off just because we both know this electricity arcing between us is wrong," she said. "Tell me how to take care of Kitty, but don't touch me. I—please."

He stepped back as if she were a hot coal. "You're right. I was wrong to touch you."

Without thinking, Delfyne turned to him. "Do not make the mistake of throwing yourself in the same category as those other men, the ones I didn't want to touch me. With you, I do. I just know I shouldn't."

So he showed her how to make Kitty comfortable. She did her best to follow his instructions. Sometimes, their hands would touch, and Delfyne's breath would catch in her throat. When they finished and she handed him the curry comb, her fingertips brushed against his. Desire rushed through her, and she wanted to hide her hot face against Kitty's coat. But that would have told him just how much she wanted him. Because it was beyond desire, she knew. Her emotions ran much deeper, and stronger, and that was something she couldn't let him know.

So she squared her shoulders and forced a smile. "I'd better wash up and help Lydia."

As if on cue, the phone rang. The stable phone was connected to the house line. Delfyne jumped, and the phone stopped ringing. Someone had answered it inside the house.

"Delfyne, what's going on? Why are you so nervous?"

"Oh my goodness, Delfyne help me." Lydia suddenly called out from the house. "I'm not even close to being ready and he's coming. For real. I didn't get started getting dressed, because I didn't think it was really going to happen."

Delfyne started toward the house at a clip. "Lydia is going on a date."

"With who?"

"Ben Whitcliff."

"That old coot?"

Delfyne whirled. "He's a very nice man, and he likes Lydia. And…" She lowered her voice. "Didn't you hear how she sounded? She likes him, too."

"But…Lydia? She's never even—"

"Done anything, because she was too busy taking care of this house and you."

She continued hurrying to the house. When she reached the kitchen door she turned to look at Owen, who'd stopped a few feet back. He was staring at her and at the house as if his entire world had suddenly turned into a giant pumpkin.

"You did this," he said softly.

"Well…not really."

His smile was slow. "Yes, really. You put it into Ben's head at the Hall, I'll bet. You encouraged him."

"Didn't you see him that day at Molly's? He didn't need very much encouragement at all," she retorted.

Suddenly Owen tipped back his head and laughed.

"Shh, Lydia will hear you," Delfyne whispered, although if she hadn't heard already it would be a miracle.

"I'm not laughing at Lydia, Delfyne. It's you. All you. I'll bet you just jumped in feetfirst and dropped blatant hints in Ben's ear, didn't you? You are a constant surprise."

"Yes, well, I've heard that before. Too many times."

And with that, she went inside. Owen shook his head as she went upstairs. Now he was probably thinking about her the way her family did. She needed a keeper. And he was right, in a way. This could all have gone so very wrong. Lydia could have been hurt. Lydia could still be hurt if this date didn't work out.

Delfyne tried not to think about that. She helped Lydia choose clothing, makeup and jewelry. Then she walked her downstairs to where Ben was now waiting.

"You have a good evening, Lydia," Delfyne said and kissed the older woman's cheek. "I mean that. It's a command."

"Are you sure you'll be all right, hon?" Lydia asked.

"I'll be perfect. I'll be very careful and I'll clean up your kitchen when I'm done. You just go have a good time with Ben," she said, eyeing the man who was looking at Lydia as if she were an apple pie and he wanted more than a slice.

Lydia was turning toward the door when Owen came downstairs. "Hello, Ben," he said. "Lydia?" The woman who had raised him looked at him very sternly.

"Owen, you be nice to Delfyne and don't demand too much. This is her first full meal with no help," Lydia told him.

"I'll relish every bite," he promised. "But you…" he said to Ben. The man finally looked away from Lydia and raised his gaze to Owen. "Just where are you taking her?" Owen asked.

"Owen!" Lydia admonished.

"I was thinking of the Ambassador Steak House in Barton," Ben said.

"Good choice," Owen said with a smile. "I didn't know you had such class." He looked at Delfyne as if approving her choice.

Delfyne beamed. Ben and Lydia shuffled around looking as nervous as two green teenagers. "Before you go, Lydia," Owen said, "let me put these on you." And he pulled a slender necklace of perfect pearls from his pocket.

Lydia looked up at him, love and shock clear in her brown eyes. "Oh, Owen, no. Those were your mother's," she protested. "You can't mean for me to wear them. What if I lost them? What if the string broke?"

Owen undid the clasp and placed the necklace around Lydia's neck. "She wasn't much of a mother, Lydia, but you were," he said. "Always." He kissed her cheek. "Have a good time tonight."

Lydia blinked, clearly fighting tears, and turned to hug him hard. "You were such a good boy. Now look, you're going to make my makeup run," she said.

"Then you'd better go," he said, his voice low. "And, Ben, don't bring her home too late and don't try any funny stuff," he warned.

"Owen!" Lydia squealed.

"I'll treat her with the greatest respect, son. I've waited a long time for this," Ben promised.

Then they were out the door.

Delfyne stared at Owen. "You are an amazing man."

He slowly shook his head. "I should have realized long ago that she deserved better than just this kitchen."

"She's happy here," Delfyne reminded him. "She loves cooking for you, and it's a very nice kitchen."

Right now it felt like a very small, steamy kitchen despite its size. "I'll have dinner ready in no time," she promised.

"What are you making?"

"Beef stew and cake. It will be edible," she told him.

It was, but just barely. Still, Owen told her that it was a wonderful meal and he ate every bite. The man was going to make her cry.

She had a terrible feeling that she was going to be crying over Owen for a long time after she left here.

CHAPTER TWELVE

HE NEEDED to put emotional brakes on, Owen told himself a few days later. His attachment to Delfyne was growing too strong. It was to the point where he hated to leave the house anymore, and he had to leave the house. He couldn't desert the men to run the ranch themselves. Already they were starting to look at him as if he had lost his senses.

What's more, going to the house and seeing her wasn't helping, because in the house he ran into Ben, who had taken to hanging around looking moon-eyed and desperate. Lydia was just as bad. Even the pregnant Timbelina looked content and homey and in love with something, even if it was just her belly and the prospect of being a mother. All that contentment when he was so discontented was driving him mad.

The truth was that, like it or not, Delfyne was going to leave soon. The days and weeks had gone flying past. He should welcome that. Life could get back to normal then. He could stop thinking about her so much.

But not today. Not yet. And every time he saw her, every time she told him she wanted to see more of his ranch he just…

"You'd think I could be happy over her enthusiasm," he found himself telling Jake and Alf as he walked, the dogs at his heels. "But you and I know about ranch virgins who are just here for the short term. That enthusiasm is selective. It's not real and… she's going, boys. I don't want her to get too attached and feel sad when she leaves."

Already he had taken her on a couple more trips with him. He'd let her pound some nails and get some grease on her hands, but the novelty of it all and her own lack of exposure to anything like the real world of work had left her entranced.

"Won't last much longer," he told the dogs. "Sooner or later she'll see a bug or a snake or end up muddy or bloody—or even worse, she'll experience the tragedy of a calf that doesn't make it, or a mother losing her baby and…"

He slammed in through the door and stuck his head in the kitchen. Lydia was nowhere to be seen. But Delfyne was definitely there. She was bent over the stove, her pretty little rounded rear end right there for him to see. Sweat broke out on his forehead just like that. Desire sluiced through his body, and he suddenly couldn't get enough air into his lungs.

But when she straightened up and turned around, she looked so sad that he forgot all about the ache to bed her. Owen was next to her in two long strides, his boots clattering on the wood of the kitchen floor. "What happened? Are you hurt?"

She blinked those entrancing violet eyes. "Owen, I—oh, nothing happened really and no, I'm not hurt. I'm just…I'm so angry." As if to demonstrate she put her hands on her hips.

"You're angry? You want to explain that?"

She held out one hand, indicating the pan on the stove. No, make that four pans. "Four times today I have attempted to make your cake, that chocolate surprise devil of a cake. And four times it's come out all wrong."

Owen felt his lips twitching. He peered around her at four cakes. One completely flat, two lop-sided and one…

"That one looks just fine to me," he said.

She closed her eyes. "It's not. It's not. It's so wrong. It's not nearly as high as Lydia's and…" She looked up and tears were in her eyes. "Andreus called," she whispered.

Owen didn't wait. He didn't ask what he wanted to ask. He just stepped forward and tugged her into his arms. He kissed her. He stroked her back. Then he kissed her again. His heart was shattering, his mind was gone, he could barely see, he was so upset, but he focused on her because she was all that mattered in this moment.

"You have to go?"

"Not yet, but…soon. He called so we could make the arrangements. I have two weeks. Just two weeks and…" She looked at the sad little cakes. "I didn't do half the things I wanted to do here."

"It's all right," he said, kissing her hair, stroking her.

And suddenly she was on her toes. She was kissing him back. "It's not all right," she whispered fervently. "Not at all. I have so many things I've planned, so many things I want to do, so many things I—I want." She kissed him again. She twined herself around him until she was almost a part of him and still he wanted more of her. He wanted to be all for her, to console her and be her shoulder. "I—oh, Owen. I want so much." She kissed his lips, his chin, the underside of his jaw.

He dragged her back up, his fingers curled in her hair as he found her mouth and tasted her deeply, fully, trying to get inside her. When he finally released her, they were both breathing hard.

"Owen, I—" A low moan escaped her. "Just look at me. I'm doing it again. That impulsive thing. Saying and doing all kinds of things without thought to who you are and who I am and what I should be doing. I'm just pulling you into my sadness when it isn't your fault at all that I have to go home soon."

"But not yet," he said. "You don't have to go yet. And a lot can still happen in two weeks if we plan carefully. So we'll do as much as we can in the short time you have left. I'll get Ben to help out around here. He knows the ropes of ranching and he pretty much lives here nowadays anyway."

Delfyne looked up at him with glowing eyes. "You'll be with me all day?"

A part of him knew he should say no. He shouldn't even have started this whole thing. When she left, he would be in too deep, she would be entwined too tightly into his life at the ranch. Her leaving would rip him apart and leave him torn.

Right now, torn seemed like a good risk. It was the only way he would have it. "All day," he said.

"What will we do?" she asked.

And for the first time today his smile was genuine in spite of the sadness that filled his heart. "Everything," he told her. "We'll do everything."

For the next three days Delfyne had almost too many things to do. The hours weren't long enough to cram in all the activities that Owen had planned for her, but this morning, Owen had insisted on a break, and the darn man felt he had good reason.

Delfyne stood on the lawn in front of the house while Owen eyed her critically. "I know what you said. You've practiced, but I need you to show me what you know," he said. "It's not enough for you to watch some videos."

Delfyne frowned. "Owen, I don't want to attack you."

He crossed his arms. "Yeah, I got that message. You've already said it three times, but let me repeat myself again. Or maybe I should rephrase it. Delfyne, Princess," he drawled in that low, sexy way that made her knees wobble and her heart ache and the rest of her go on full desire alert, so that she didn't even care that he had gone and called her *Princess* as if it were her name. "I just don't want—" he said. "No, I *can't* be stuck here half-crazy with worry that some guy's going to try something you haven't invited when I'm not there to help you. I need to know you're safe, Delfyne, so come on and do it. Please."

All right, so she just couldn't resist Owen when he asked her nicely.

She blew out a breath and shook herself to relax. "Okay, come at me as if you're going to loop your arm around me and choke me."

"Like this?" He loosely slung his arm around her neck from behind. Now his skin lay against hers. She breathed in the scent of him for a second. She felt his heartbeat against her back.

And his touch was…gentle, not the touch of an attacker. "Delfyne?" he said in a voice that didn't sound a thing like that of a man who wanted to steal her bag.

She shook her head. *Focus, focus*, she told herself. This wasn't about her and Owen. It couldn't be. Neither of them wanted it to be.

"You have to seem like you really mean to hurt me," she commanded.

He tightened his hold slightly. She touched the corded muscles in his arm and pushed a little, but he didn't let go.

"Attack me," he said. "Protect yourself. Push me away. Do it."

Yes. She had to. Not just because she needed to protect herself from caring too much, but because she knew that he really was going to worry if she couldn't show him that she'd never again become some man's potential victim.

"All right, I bring my elbow down into your side," she said, her voice strong. She demonstrated the move but didn't make full contact. "Then I tuck my chin so you can't choke me any more, I grab your arm firmly with both hands, stomp on your instep as hard as I can, and shove your arm forward to free myself while turning and side-kicking hard into your groin." She moved as she spoke, showing him what she'd learned, moving fluidly.

"Good. You've practiced a lot," he said. "What else?"

"Well, if that doesn't work, I tuck my chin and drop my body completely so that my weight drags my opponent off balance. Then I shove back hard with my hips, using as much force as I can manage. The trick is to throw him off balance so that I can break free and get away."

"But you haven't tried it in a real situation," he mused.

Delfyne closed her eyes and shook her head. "No, and, Owen, don't even ask me to try. I've forced myself to memorize all the moves, to learn to use my brain to figure out what my weapons would be in such a situation, but I will *not* attempt to hurt you or throw you. Don't ask me to. What if I did throw you and you broke something? How do you think I would feel about that? Just trust me, please. I've never forgotten that fear of having a man turn on me. I *know* I would do what was necessary. I've lived my whole life learning and training to do whatever is necessary, and when the time comes I'll do it."

And suddenly they weren't talking about self-defense anymore.

She looked up at him, pleading with her eyes. "I understand what's required," she said. "Even if I don't want to think about it."

Owen swore. "Well, you're not going to have to think about it. At least not today. We're going to visit the parts of the ranch you haven't yet seen. Plan for an overnight trip. For the rest of today you don't have to think of anything but being yourself."

Delfyne's heart filled as she looked into his eyes. She wanted to throw her arms around his neck, but instead she just smiled and gave him a very inadequate, "Thank you. I'll get ready."

Soon they were bumping along the road in the Land Rover, headed for the far reaches of the Second Chance.

"It's such an energizing place, your ranch," she couldn't help saying.

Owen's face was transformed by a wry smile as he drove. "That's an interesting way to describe it. What do you mean by that?"

"I don't know. Some parts of it are very stark, but some parts are bold, almost too much even to take in, with towering pines and the mountains looming in the distance. But all of it is open and so big. It's a bit like taking a constricting garment off and finally taking a really deep breath of air."

A low, masculine chuckle had Delfyne turning toward Owen. "I didn't mean it to be funny."

"It wasn't. It was…I don't know. Right, I guess."

But as the day passed and they hiked and picnicked, waded through the creek and traced the outer edges of the Second Chance as the sun began to set, Owen looked less than happy.

"Night's coming soon," he said.

"I know. It does tend to follow day."

But he didn't laugh. "Out here, night tends to emphasize how alone a person is. It folds you into a cocoon and shuts you off from the world. Mostly I like the feeling, but alone with you and cut off from the world, with darkness all around…" He shook his head. "Coming out here with you and staying this late was a bad idea," he said. "I know what I promised, but I must have been crazy to think it would be okay. I should take you back to the house."

Delfyne knew what he meant. The dark made everything more private and personal and tempting, and Owen was already far too tempting. She itched to touch him all the time already. Fighting her desire was a constant trial. "You're right. We should go. But…" She frowned and sighed. "If we do go back to the house…"

"What?"

"Well, I told Lydia and Ben that I wouldn't be home tonight and…"

Owen rubbed one hand over his jaw. "Are you telling me that if I go home I'm liable to walk in on Lydia and Ben…having sex?"

"Oh, well, I think it's love. They would be making love, Owen." But she couldn't keep the smile from her face.

"Damn, Delfyne, why did you have to go and tell me about that? There are just certain things that a man doesn't want to know about…about…"

"A woman who is like a mother to him," she finished. "Yes, I know. That is, I can't be sure they would be doing that. It's not really like Lydia, but…"

"But I'll bet it's just like Ben. He probably couldn't wait for us to leave."

"I wouldn't know about that. Actually, it's good that he's there, isn't it? You wouldn't want her to be alone at night."

Owen made a grumbling sound. "No. I wouldn't, but…"

"Owen, look, see the moon?" Delfyne pointed upward, and, of course, Owen looked. "It's so very beautiful here tonight," she whispered. "Your ranch is amazing, Owen."

To her surprise he didn't answer right away. When he finally did, it was with a dull look of resignation in his eyes. "I know exactly what you mean. I've witnessed this phenomenon before. A visitor comes here, and everything they see is amazing at first, yes. This is a totally exciting and *different* world from what they're used to. But different gets old when it goes on for too long."

She knew that by *different* he meant this land and the demands of his world, but…people had told her all her life that *she* was different. Maybe it worked that way with people, too. Maybe after he'd known her for a while, her mystique and entertainment value would wear off and he'd want someone more like the women he'd always known. He'd realize that he preferred women who didn't do silly, impulsive things and who didn't need to have keepers watching over them so that they wouldn't do something foolish.

So, when he urged her back into the SUV and took off down

the road, she didn't say anything at first. Until the tension and the not knowing what was to come got to be too much for her. "Are we going back to the house, then?" she asked.

"Not if Lydia's in the middle of a romantic interlude. No, there's a building not far from here. At one time, there was a line shack there, but it was falling down, so I had it removed and a new structure put up. It's a good place for the men and their wives to go for mini-vacations when they don't have enough time or money to get away. It's fully stocked."

She stared at him in the deepening shadows, noting how the last pink rays of light turned his face into hard, virile lines that made her ache. Which was just too bad. It was clear that he was already regretting this outing, or at least this part of it.

"You're good to your men. It's nice that they have a place to go."

"They work hard. They should have options. This is just one."

But she had no options, and Owen had no options.

A sigh escaped her, and Owen turned to stare at her, but the growing darkness obscured his features and he said nothing. Soon they came to the house. It was small but sturdy and, as he said, well-equipped.

They set up, made dinner, cleaned up, all with a peculiar tense sort of silence. Finally, when all that was done and there was nothing left to do, she followed Owen onto the porch. He stood leaning against one of the porch rails, looking up, but she got the feeling that he wasn't seeing a thing.

Letting the door shut softly behind her, she moved next to him. "You brought me out here to show me your ranch, and now you're regretting it."

"Yes."

"Why?"

"Because…" He slammed the flat of his hand against the rail. "I thought I could just do this last good thing, be an entertaining host, play the good-guy friend and send you back, but you're here and I'm here and…"

He turned to her. "I don't want to be one of those men who knows you have a date with destiny but who still tries to take advantage of you."

She looked at him solemnly. "You haven't even touched me today."

His laugh was harsh. "Yes, and I have the fingernail marks in my palms to show for it. I want to touch you. I want more than that."

"And so do I."

He didn't say anything, but he came close. He cupped her face in his big palms. She knew he was going to kiss her. She also knew that he was never going to do more. He would send her home untouched despite the fingernail marks in his palms because that was the kind of honorable man that he was. He would fight his desire and wrestle it to the ground like a bull at a rodeo.

But she was different. As always. She and her future husband hadn't announced their engagement, but they would. They hadn't even kissed, though she knew they would do that soon, too.

So, although she still had more than a week before she had to leave, Delfyne knew that tonight was it. Once she left America she would become a bride-to-be, an engaged, committed and faithful one. And after tonight, Owen would never risk this kind of closeness again. The two of them would begin the business of disentangling their lives. All she had was tonight. This was all that was left.

"Owen," she whispered.

He kissed her.

"Owen, I don't want just kisses. I want to be under the stars with you. I want to make love with you."

He kissed her again. Slowly. Sweetly. Pulling her heart from her. "I can't do that to you."

"Owen…yes. Please, do that to me."

He groaned and dragged her up against him, her body molded to his. "I can't think of anything I want more, but I'm fighting it, and—"

She slipped her hand up and covered his lips. When he was still, she replaced her fingertips with her mouth, then pulled away.

"When I leave here, I lose my choice," she told him. "The man I'll marry was chosen for me, the man I'll make love with for the rest of my life was chosen for me. I'll be a creature of duty and only duty. That's the way it must be. But tonight…let me choose you, Owen. Please. Give me that much. Let my first time be with a man I know and truly want. I won't ask for more."

"Delfyne." His voice came out strangled and thick. "He damn well better be good to you. He'd better never mistreat you."

And without another word, he lifted her into his arms, pulling her close as he kissed her.

She laid her palm against his chest and returned his kiss.

"Open the door," he told her and once she had done that and he had carried her inside, he put her down.

They stood there locked in each other's arms as he tasted her, nipping at her lips, kissing her cheeks and her eyelids and then returning to feast on her lips again.

"You have a bed?" she asked, even though she knew exactly where the bed was. "Take me there, and don't give me any of that 'yes, Princess,' teasing that you do when I give you orders."

He smiled against her lips, but he obliged by waltzing her backward to the bed. "No, Princess, I wouldn't do that tonight," he teased.

Once she was beneath him on the bed, however, he braced his arms so that he wasn't touching her at all.

"If this is our only time, I intend to make it right. I'll be careful," he promised.

But she was already rising up and kissing as much of him as she could reach. "Don't be careful. Be you."

His response was to sweep his hand slowly up her side, tracing her curves. Every nerve ending she possessed went wild. "If you change your mind, tell me," he whispered. "I mean it, Delfyne. You scream, you push, you yell, you swear at me if you must or use those fancy new self-defense moves you've learned. Whatever it takes to get my attention, you do it and don't worry about hurting me. If you decide you don't want this after all, I'm stopping no matter how far gone I am."

She opened her mouth to protest, but he shut her up with one kiss. Then he unfastened the first button on her blouse. For several seconds he just stared at the flesh he had revealed. Then he kissed her right where that button had been.

Her heart skipped more than one beat.

He slipped another button from its place, kissing farther down. And then another. And another. Slowly, with heat and incredible patience. He drove her mad.

Then, still not finished, he stopped. She looked up to find his gaze on her as he studied her. She knew what he was thinking.

"No, I haven't changed my mind and I won't," she somehow managed to whisper, though her entire body was trembling.

"Good. If you did—" he flicked open the last button "—it just might kill me to stop."

With that, he lifted her high against him. He kissed her body as he removed every remaining stitch of her clothing.

She ripped at his shirt, much less careful than he. "Help me," she said, so he shrugged free of the cloth. He unzipped his jeans and stepped out of them. Then he slipped his big palms around her sides, his skin sliding against hers as he lowered her to the bed.

Delfyne placed her palms on his chest, feeling his racing heartbeat. "Kiss me," she commanded. "Kiss me everywhere."

He kissed her belly, and she felt his smile against her skin.

"I'll kiss you everywhere. We'll do everything," he promised. And he proceeded to kiss her in places she didn't know a person could be kissed. She was half out of her mind when he paused.

"What?" she demanded, her breath coming out ragged. "What?"

"I'm not going on to the next stage unless you're ready." His voice was so rough and halting that she could barely make out his words. The cords in his arms were standing out, but he was holding back. "You have to give the command."

"Yes. I want you to," she said, clutching at him. "I'm ready, and, oh, Owen, I ache for you. Show me the next stage. Show me now."

Without a word and gazing into her eyes the whole time, Owen came inside her, his breath hitching. He held himself still and closed his eyes for a second. Then he brought his mouth to hers. "This is the next stage, Princess. I'll stop the ache. I'll make everything right."

Then he stopped talking. He just…loved her, completely, and he was as good as his word. He was just plain amazing.

Delfyne wrapped her arms around him. She gave kiss for kiss. She had thought she knew what making love was about, but then he sent her toppling over a cliff into a world of brilliant stars and heat and sensation she'd never imagined. And when he went rigid in her arms and cried out her name, she felt powerful and special and cherished as never before.

What's more, when her breathing finally became less shallow and she was lying satisfied and happy and contented, with Owen's big body wrapped around hers, Delfyne knew that nothing in her life would ever again be as right as this one moment.

She'd fallen in love with Owen, a man forbidden to her. Life had suddenly changed…and yet it hadn't changed at all. Owen still had demons that kept him from committing, and she still had her duty to tend to. She couldn't stop being a princess just because she was in love.

CHAPTER THIRTEEN

OWEN woke with sunlight streaming in through the window, the knowledge that he had touched heaven and that he was in love with Delfyne.

Maybe he'd known that before, but this morning, raw and too aware that he had crossed a line he shouldn't have crossed, one Delfyne would surely someday regret crossing, he acknowledged the truth. He had no defenses to help him hide from it.

He had fallen in love with a princess, the one woman he could never have.

And now…

"I'll take you home," he said.

She was already up, sitting by the window looking out at the creek that ran by the cabin. She turned when he spoke and just…gazed at him.

"Thank you," she said. "For everything. But yes, I must go home now."

And that was that.

"I'm taking you in my own plane. Don't even consider arguing with me," he told her. "I promised Andreus that I would protect you and I'm going to do that. Once you're back on Xenoran soil and I've explained to Andreus why you're home early, then we'll say our goodbyes."

She opened her mouth, probably to let him know that she was capable of taking care of herself, but in the end she nodded.

It was amazing how quickly things could move forward once a man's mind went on autopilot and he turned off his emotions. Before the day was out, Delfyne was packed. She had said her goodbyes to everyone on the ranch. She'd called Nancy and Molly and even Angus and wished them well. She'd curried Kitty once more, given the reluctant Timbelina a kiss and Jake and Alf a nice scratch behind the ears. Then she and her bodyguards had climbed on board Owen's airplane.

Owen didn't allow himself to think or feel. He walled off his emotions and closed his mind to everything except making sure Delfyne was comfortable on the airplane. He concentrated on getting there and not on anything beyond or behind.

Only when the plane touched down in Xenora and they were escorted to the royal palace did his emotions begin to play games with him.

"This is where you grew up," he said as the car pulled up to the palace drive and he saw the huge, imposing white stone structure situated on a hilltop with the blue and white Xenoran flag waving. "I'd forgotten how very…palatial it is."

She touched his hand. He fought the urge to grab her, toss her back in the airplane and fly away with her to someplace where only the two of them existed.

"I don't think I realized how different it was from everyone else's life until I was much older," she admitted as two servants stepped forward and threw open the doors and they entered the palace. "I thought that everyone lived in rooms that were stiff and pristine and…"

"Exquisite," he said, supplying the word. "You don't have to apologize for who you are or try to make things seem less regal than they are. It's a beautiful palace." It wasn't stuffy, either. The crystal and gold that was everywhere was still understated. The priceless tapestries were awe-inspiring.

And Delfyne's parents, King Fyodor and Queen Melaina, who joined Andreus to greet him, were stately but warm individuals who remembered Owen from his only visit.

"It's so good to see you again," Melaina said, holding out her hand. "Our Delfyne can be quite a handful, so we appreciate your taking the time and trouble to see to her safety."

"Yes, and you're looking very lean and fit, Owen, isn't he, Andreus? Delfyne must have kept him running," Fyodor said.

Andreus laughed. "Owen always did stay in shape," he said, but he kept looking from Delfyne to Owen. Delfyne had yet to say anything other than hello to her parents and brother. Ah, she was already back in regal mode, Owen supposed. Maybe already regretting what had happened between them in the cabin. He wasn't going to let her beat herself up about that or worry that he would ever reveal her secret.

"Delfyne was a treasured guest," Owen said. "We all enjoyed her visit and we'll miss her."

He had meant for his words to reassure Delfyne and her parents, but he was so aware of Delfyne just a few feet away and yet lost to him forever that the pleasantry came out stiff.

"Owen was the perfect host," Delfyne said, but her words, too, sounded wrong. Almost as if she didn't mean them.

Owen couldn't stop himself from looking at her, but she was looking away. Of course, that was as it should be. The days at the ranch were past, and they had to move on. The fact that he felt as if he had been ripped apart inside couldn't matter.

"Well," Melaina was saying. "Let's let Owen go to his rooms and get settled in. Later tonight, we're having a gathering to celebrate Delfyne's homecoming," she told him. "As soon as we got word that you were coming, we sent out invitations. And don't worry if you didn't come prepared for a celebration, that's all taken care of. Andreus has seen to it. It will be small, anyway. Only about two hundred guests. Family, of course, and Prince Arian and his family and various other dignitaries and friends."

Delfyne hadn't actually gasped at Prince Arian's name, Owen didn't think, but in some strange way, he seemed to feel her reaction. Or maybe he just knew that she hadn't had time to prepare herself. He turned in time to see her look of shock.

"I hadn't realized I would be seeing Arian so soon," she said, her voice calm, her eyes anything but.

Fyodor smiled. "It was to be a surprise, but now you're here, he's here, and the time for surprises is past."

"It's been two years since you've really seen him, dear," her mother said. "It is time."

Delfyne looked at Owen as if she needed him to help her. Owen was already taking a step toward her, but then she closed her eyes briefly and raised her chin. When she opened her eyes again, determination and resignation were written in her expression. Owen could almost see her ordering herself to do her duty and to do it with the grace of a princess who had known her fate all her life. "Of course," she said.

She would have her reunion with her prince, the man who would wed her and bed her and provide her with little princes and princesses. Her time in Montana would soon be a distant memory.

Owen forced a smile. "I—thank you for the gracious invitation, but I'm afraid I have to get back to the ranch. I only came to escort your daughter safely home."

Immediately, a chorus of protests arose. "Please, we can't be such ungracious hosts. One night of your time. Just one."

Owen's gaze met Delfyne's, but she looked like a princess now, and he couldn't read her expression.

Later, he didn't remember acquiescing. He didn't remember much except the need to end this quickly. Nonetheless, a scant few hours later, he was in a tuxedo with Andreus by his side as they prepared to descend to meet the guests below.

"Delfyne seems different," Andreus said. "And so do you."

"You haven't seen me in a long time."

"I don't need to see in order to sense. We laughed the last time we talked. You're not laughing now."

"Travel is tiring."

"And my sister can try a man's patience. She can be annoying and a pest and a bundle of trouble."

Owen turned to his friend. "Whatever you're doing, stop doing it. You know I'm not going to criticize your sister."

Andreus smiled slightly. "Maybe you'd like to compliment her, then?"

"What are you saying, Andreus?"

His friend smiled. "Just trying to figure out why both you and Delfyne have tried to avoid looking at each other and why both of you seem tense. This is perhaps indelicate but…I have a right to ask. Did you…"

"Did I what?" Owen didn't bother to hide the edge in his voice.

Andreus shoved one impatient hand through his hair. "You're like a brother to me, Owen, but Delfyne is my sister. If I thought you had hurt her in some way I would…"

"Not do more to me than I would do to myself," Owen said. And then the air finally went out of him and he let the tension drain away. "I would never hurt her, Dré. This trip was a mistake. I just wanted to see her safely home. Now…I can't stay. I mean that. I really can't stay, so as soon as I go downstairs and meet your guests, you're going to make sure I get an emergency call. Then I'm leaving. I can't be here."

Andreus moved up in front of his friend. "You're as good as

any of the guests. At least you're as rich as any of them and you're a lot nicer than some of them."

"Not happening, buddy," Owen said. "Thank you. I love you like a brother, and your parents are wonderful people, but I'm going."

"You have it bad, don't you?"

Owen didn't even pretend to misunderstand what Andreus was saying, but he wasn't going to confirm or discuss his feelings for Delfyne with anyone, especially not Dré.

"Come on, let's go meet the royals."

"Owen, do not let my parents hear you call our guests by that term," Andreus warned. "They don't like it."

"All right, understood. So, what do they call their royal guests?"

Andreus grinned. "They call some of them fools."

And for the first time all day Owen actually laughed. But he knew it wouldn't last. In less than an hour, he'd be saying goodbye to Delfyne forever.

Delfyne couldn't help searching the room for Owen. It was all she could do to keep from pacing in the long ice-blue gown that felt too low-cut and uncomfortable compared to the jeans she had grown used to. But it wasn't the dress that was really bothering her. Andreus had slipped up beside her and let her know that Owen was leaving after dinner. She didn't want him to go without saying goodbye. She didn't want him to go at all.

But before Owen could appear, Prince Arian arrived. He was much handsomer than she remembered but in a very pretty and polished way, she couldn't help thinking. She just couldn't imagine him in jeans, with his shirt hanging open after a hard day of work, or with the sun turning his skin golden or the moon lighting his eyes.

Automatically she curtseyed deeply. She offered her hand. He kissed it and smiled at her just as Owen and Andreus came in at the other end of the hall.

Her gaze locked with Owen's, and for a minute the whole huge room disappeared. She could hear Prince Arian talking, but she didn't know what he was saying. Nor did she care.

Andreus pulled on Owen's sleeve and the two of them moved off.

"The ranching life, what was it like?" Arian was saying.

Delfyne tried to smile at the man who was, after all, only being polite. "It was an illuminating experience," she said, veering toward the vague. The truth was that she didn't want to share too much about the ranch with a stranger. Not yet. She needed time to hold her memories close before she let them go for good.

He wrinkled his nose. "I wouldn't like it. All that mess. Dirt. Sweat. Smells. And all those animals."

"Maybe you'd like it if you tried it. I had a cat," she said, attempting to find common ground.

"A cat? No. Ugh. I hate them. *We* won't have any, I assure you."

Delfyne raised a brow. "Timbelina was a pretty cat."

"Timebelina?"

"That's what I named her." She explained why.

He laughed and chucked her under the chin. *Actually chucked her under the chin.* "You're such a child. I like that. It's refreshing that you're so naive. But no cats, no matter how sweet you are. I'll give you babies instead. Lots of babies to keep you busy. If I give you something to do, you won't care about animals anymore. You'll like the babies I give you, won't you? I remember you used to like dolls."

Delfyne resisted the urge to hit him. As if a baby was something one bought at a store to appease a woman. "I was eight when I liked dolls. We haven't spent a lot of time together over the years."

"But we will," he said with a grin. "We'll soon be married and you'll learn to like me. In my bed, I'll make you squeal. You'll learn what pleases me." He placed his hand over hers.

A wave of something very much like fear washed over Delfyne. She had a strong desire to use a self-defense maneuver on him. But that would be wrong. Arian was to be her husband. He had the right to say what he was saying. There was no need to feel so claustrophobic and ill and…

"I do *not* squeal," she said without thinking. And then she turned. "Forgive me. I hope you'll excuse me. I don't feel well." Without waiting for him to answer, she fled.

But to where? Where was Owen? She needed to see him. He was leaving. Too soon. Andreus had said so. Would he go without even saying goodbye? She'd never see him again after this. The very thought made her stumble, but she kept moving and searching, the panic building inside her.

Rushing out into the hall, she found him with Andreus and stopped short.

Without taking her eyes off Owen, she touched her brother's hand. "I love you, Andreus," she told him. "I've missed seeing you, and we haven't even had a chance to talk yet, but…we'll talk later. Right now, you need to leave. I really mean that."

There was a long moment of silence. Finally, she looked at Andreus. He raised a brow, opened his mouth to say something.

She gave him a look they'd shared as children. It meant *I will make you pay later if you thwart me now.* Andreus had been the master of the look. He'd invented it, but Delfyne did a pretty good job now. Without so much as another glance, he whisked himself away.

"Andreus told me that you were going," she said to Owen, rushing in, her words spilling out fast. "You're leaving right now, aren't you? This very minute? You weren't even going to say goodbye to me."

Without a word he stepped forward and brushed one finger down her cheek. He shook his head. "You're wrong. I was determined to say goodbye. I was simply waiting for the right moment."

"Is this it?"

"You know the answer. I can't stay."

"It's because of your ranch, isn't it? Of course. I should have thought of that before now. I shouldn't have let you fly me home. You're needed there."

"Delfyne," he said gently, and she thought her heart would break into two ragged pieces.

This wouldn't do. Owen had known such guilt in his life. Letting him see how his departure was tearing at her would only make him hate himself. She couldn't let him see her cry, so she struggled for a smile and even managed a somewhat tremulous one. "Besides, who knows what Ben and Lydia are up to with no one there to chaperone them?" she asked, trying to make the ending moment light.

It worked…for a second. Owen smiled, too. "Lydia and Ben? They're probably doing this," he said, and he gently kissed her. "Goodbye, Princess. You're the best guest the Second Chance ever had. I won't ever forget you."

And then he turned and walked out the door and out of her life. The clicking of the door snapping shut and separating her from him sent Delfyne into full panic mode.

She ran to the door and opened it. "Owen," she cried. But when he turned, she didn't know what to say. What could she say? *Don't go? I love you? Don't leave me?* No, she couldn't say any of those things because saying the words would only make the truth harder to bear.

"Have Lydia write me to let me know when Timbelina has her babies," she said.

He gazed at her for so long that for just a few seconds she felt some sort of sad and foolish hope that the two of them could stay there staring at each other forever.

"The minute it happens," he finally said, and this time when he left, she closed the door on him and her hopes. Ten minutes later, Andreus found her there on her knees on the carpet sobbing uncontrollably.

He dropped down beside her and took her into his arms.

"Fyna, please don't cry. You're breaking my heart," he told her, using her childhood nickname. "I should never have sent you to Owen."

Despite her tears, Delfyne shook her head. She touched his face gently. "He was the best gift you ever gave me, Dré. Thank you."

Then she struggled to her feet and went to her room. When she rose the next morning, she was composed, if devoid of life. It was time to do her duty.

CHAPTER FOURTEEN

OWEN stared at the cat sitting at his feet just inside the front door. Timbelina was whimpering—actually whimpering—and looking at him as if he needed to do something to make her world better.

He had never paid much attention to cats. They were just there, a necessary part of the ranch. But this one had caught Delfyne's attention, and she would be worried if the pregnancy didn't go according to plan. And darn it…the cat was crying! He just couldn't ignore that.

"Cat…Timbelina," he said, not even looking around to see if anyone was listening. "You are going to be the best-cared-for cat Montana has ever known, and it's not just going to be this bed Delfyne made for you. When you have those kittens, and Lydia writes Delfyne to tell her about it, I want her to hear only good things, and…I'd even send her one of your kittens so she would miss you less, but I wouldn't want to quarantine the poor little thing. Besides, Delfyne would be beside herself if she thought she was taking away one of your babies."

The cat tilted her head as if she understood. She whimpered again, and suddenly Owen's heart just hurt so much he could barely stand it. He had to get away from this terrible pain. "Stay healthy, cat," he said, as he stumbled through the screen door, letting it bounce shut behind him with a series of small bangs.

And then he was practically running for…he had no idea what. Work. Working until he was ready to drop was the only way he could make it through the day.

"Owen!" Lydia's voice brought him up short. He turned.

"You can't live like this," Lydia said. "I'm worried about her. You have to call her. You love her. Don't deny it."

He wasn't about to. He would never deny Delfyne. "She's a princess, Lydia. I never told you that. I couldn't tell you while she was here. She wanted everyone to treat her like a normal person, but…now, she's marrying a prince. It's over." He turned back around.

"I know she's a princess," Lydia said, and her voice, though soft, still carried. "I know how to use that Google thing, too, and I found out. Heck, I bet just about everyone in town knew and kept the secret. Delfyne being a princess doesn't make a difference to your heart, though. Love can work miracles, Owen."

He knew that, because love had done what nothing else had ever done for him. He'd spent years thinking that the reason he hadn't been able to hold his wife or to give another woman what she needed and wanted was because he had an essential character flaw, that he was incapable of being the kind of man to love truly and deeply enough. But being with Delfyne had taught him that he could be that man who cared enough to give it all. If there was a chance in the world that he could be with her, the *where* would no longer matter. Montana would be just a memory if it didn't suit her. A plain wooden box of a cabin with just the basics would be enough for him if she was there with him. The crowds of the city would be all right, too. Delfyne had taught him that he wasn't flawed. His heart had just been waiting to be fully awakened, and he hadn't realized it. He could love enough to give with Delfyne, and if her situation were different…

"I know love can change things, Lydia," he said. "But this time it can't. If I tried to make her mine, I would harm her. This just isn't going to happen."

And he had darn well better get used to learning to live without her. He would do that, too. He would at least start trying to forget her.

As Lydia opened the door to go back inside, he looked at the cat. The poor animal was looking for Delfyne, wasn't it? Was Delfyne missing Timbelina, too? It occurred to him that Delfyne had had many of the things she'd loved yanked away from her. That was just wrong.

So what are you going to do about that? he asked himself. *Is there anything you can do?*

"Well if there is, I'm doing it," he promised himself aloud. "We'll just call it a wedding present."

Delfyne was in her room when there was a light knock on the door. She opened it to find Andreus standing there, holding a big box.

She frowned in confusion as he held the box out to her. "What's this?"

"I don't know. I just know that I received a call from Owen yesterday. He had a lot of questions. Do you have any pets? Are you practicing your self-defense moves? Are you happy?"

Delfyne's heart clenched. "Owen called and you didn't tell me? You didn't call me to the telephone?" She tried to keep the panic from her voice.

"He wouldn't let me. It was a very short conversation, but one of the servants just brought this to me. It arrived this morning, and he wasn't sure if it was all right for you to accept a package from your *American*, as he put it."

Anticipation and...something else, something painful, filled

Delfyne's soul as she sank to her knees, holding the box. Her hands shook, and she couldn't manage to tear the tape.

"Let me," Andreus said, his voice gentle as he assisted her.

The box flaps gave way, and Delfyne reached inside. When she looked up there was a small smile on her face and tears in her eyes.

"What is it, Fyna?" Andreus said.

"Oh…wonderful stuff. Some recipes from Lydia. Photos of Timbelina and Jake and Alf and Lydia and…oh, of everyone I knew there. There's a—a note from Owen. He says that the townspeople decided that the wood-products people weren't right for the town but that they've got a new business that makes green products. And…and he says he wishes he could send me a kitten but he wasn't sure I could keep one in the castle. He says everyone misses me." Her voice dropped to a whisper, she stumbled over her words and had to stop talking.

"Is there a photo of Owen?"

She looked up at him with sad eyes as she struggled to speak. "No, but…I'm not surprised. Owen wouldn't think it was right for me to have a picture of a man when I'm marrying someone else."

"I know," he said solemnly. "That's a big box for a few photos."

She bit her lip. "That's because it's full of bracelets. Hundreds of the bracelets he knows I love," she whispered, holding up one that was made of pink and white and gold hearts strung together.

"Hearts," Andreus said. "Owen, the least demonstrative man I know, gave you hearts."

"Dré…he gave me so much more than hearts," Delfyne said, but when she looked up at Andreus and saw the worry in his eyes she shook her head. "Don't be concerned. It doesn't mean anything. It can't mean anything. You know that."

But as she sat there, hugging the box to herself after Andreus had gone, her tears fell on the heart bracelet she had tangled in her fingers. She realized that this bracelet wasn't inexpensive plastic, and there was an engraving on the back of the largest heart, the golden one. "Your happiness is all that matters," it said.

She pressed the metal to her lips and kissed it. "No, yours matters more, so I have to be strong for your sake," she whispered to the man who would never hear her words.

Someday she would send him a photo to prove she was unharmed and content, so that he would be happy...but she couldn't do that yet. She was afraid that the look in her eyes would reveal too much of the truth.

Delfyne heard her parents and Andreus whispering as she passed the library. They'd done a lot of that during the three days since her return. In times gone by, she might have at least cared what they were saying about her, but lately the answers didn't matter.

"Delfyne," her mother called. "We want to talk to you."

Delfyne entered the room. Her parents and Andreus were lined up, looking like some sort of royal inquisition. Somehow her curiosity wasn't piqued. She just couldn't care.

"What is going on with you and Arian, Delfyne?" her father asked. "I need to know what all the fuss is about."

That caught her by surprise. "Nothing," she said carefully. "I haven't made a fuss. I see him every day. I'm going to marry him just as you planned."

Her father huffed. "That's it, then, Melaina, you're right. Something's wrong."

Delfyne blinked. Her mother stepped forward and took her hands. "Something *is* wrong. You don't laugh with Arian. Ever. And...your father is right. The fact that you're doing just what *we* planned says a lot. Delfyne...you always fuss and do a few foolish things before settling in to your duty. The fact that you're not...Andreus told us that you received a package from America. Delfyne, what did that man do to you?"

There was no point in even pretending she didn't understand who "that man" was. "He let me name his cat. And…he found a horse for me that was so gentle I couldn't possibly be scared. He let me use his kitchen and he ate what I cooked and lied and told me it was good and…"

She couldn't help it. A tear ran down her cheek.

"Delfyne, you're crying," he father said. "You never cry."

"Except for the past three nights," Andreus said. "I've heard you when I pass your room."

"Oh, Delfyne, do you hate Arian so much?" her mother asked.

"No. I don't, but he…he said that I couldn't have a cat. He said he'd make sure I had lots of babies, instead. And I—oh, I don't hate him. I just don't like him very much."

"Oh, Delfyne," her mother said, taking her in her arms.

"Tell them about the self-defense lessons," Andreus said.

Delfyne blinked and Melaina released her. "Owen told you?" she asked her brother. "What else did he tell you?"

Andreus was practically seething. "He told me, and yes, he told me why. He didn't like breaking your trust, but he insisted that I screen my friends more carefully."

Delfyne's heart broke a little more. What was Owen doing now, she wondered?

"What?" she said when she realized that her father was talking to her.

"Your brother just told me that some of our guests have tried to seduce you, even forcefully," Fyodor said, bristling. "Delfyne, who were these people who tried to hurt you?"

She shook her head. "It was long ago, Father. And it wouldn't happen now. Owen made sure I could protect myself. Owen hit a man who tried to touch me and threw him off his ranch, and Owen also—"

The words wouldn't come out, her lips were trembling so.

"Delfyne," her mother said gently. "You're a princess."

"Do you think I don't know that? It's the reason I can't be with the man I love." The tears were falling harder now.

"And if you weren't a princess?" her father asked.

Delfyne wanted to say that everything would be fine, but…

"I don't know. There are lots of women who want him, and he doesn't want anyone. He's married to his ranch, and I don't think he'll ever want children after losing his son."

"So, even if you were free, he might never marry you," her mother said.

Delfyne couldn't deny that. "But I'd still love him," she whispered. "And I wouldn't dishonor that love by marrying someone I don't love or even like."

Her father smiled in that gentle way he sometimes had when he was going to say something instructive. "You've seen your sisters and Andreus follow their duties, and you know the restrictions of a royal life. But it's also a safe life in many ways. You've been shielded from the risks of an ordinary life. I wonder if you know just how painful life like that can be."

"You're right. I don't know, but…is it worse than not caring if you get up in the morning because the person you love most is far away? Is it worse than worrying about him every minute and feeling as if the years ahead of you seem empty because he won't ever be there?" she wondered. "Is it—" Her voice broke. "—is it worse than being afraid that he might get hurt and you wouldn't even have the right to go to him because you had been married off to someone else for political gain?"

A sob broke from her mother. "Fyodor!" Melaina cried. "Do something."

Delfyne went to her, her own tears streaming as she gathered her mother close. "I'm sorry, Mother. I shouldn't have said all that. Believe me, I don't want to hurt you. It serves no purpose for me to complain, because there's nothing Father can do, anyway. I am who I am, I was born to this purpose, and promises have been made. There are expectations, commitments and… centuries of history. Contracts have been signed."

The clock ticked loudly. A sadness settled over all of them. No one spoke.

"I can't," Fyodor said, holding out his hands helplessly. "The scandal…and this man you want…a man you barely know, who calls Andreus to ask about you—which is completely inappropriate in your situation—a divorced man who has already told you that he doesn't feel that he can commit to a woman…"

His words trailed off, but then he shook his head. "To send you to that…no, I can't. You're right. There's nothing I can or will do. You'll be happy with Arian, eventually."

Delfyne was expecting no less or any more than that, and this conversation was only leaving deeper wounds. She gave an almost imperceptible nod, fighting more tears as she struggled to get to the door.

"Delfyne," Andreus said. "Not yet."

"I have to have a moment," she said, her voice tear-choked and desperate. "Please."

But he didn't listen. Instead he walked up beside her. He took her hand. "There may be nothing Father can do," he said, "but *you* can."

She shook her head, confused.

Andreus drifted nearer. "You told me the other day that Arian said you were acting like a child. Be a child," he said. "Remember."

She turned to see her parents looking at each other.

"Vondiver," Andreus whispered loudly enough for his voice to carry.

"Oh no," Fyodor said. "That is a madman's path. There's no

turning back and only utter ruination if she tries it and things fall apart."

But Delfyne was looking at her mother, and her mother wasn't cringing. "Vondiver," Delfyne said softly, referring to the child's story that had entranced her and Andreus and their siblings when they had been young and impressionable. "He gave up his crown to follow the woman he loved around the world."

"But he lost her," her mother said. "He went insane."

"Yes." Delfyne knew that. The story wasn't real, but it had been her favorite. "He lost her, anyway."

"Are you even sure he loves you?" Fyodor asked, and now his voice sounded fearful. "Don't risk this, Delfyne. Andreus, why did you even suggest this? At least she knows what she's getting with Arian."

Yes, she knew.

"And he at least will give you babies." Fyodor pressed on. "Delfyne, it's just a story. Don't be irresponsible or rash. Wait a while. We'll postpone the announcement of your engagement for three months. Then, if you decide you still can't love Arian, we'll manage to find someone more to your liking. Someone suitable."

"Or…at least call your Owen to make sure he'll have you. Yes, do that," her mother said.

But Delfyne saw the flaw in that plan. Owen would never allow Delfyne to abdicate for him. Even to ask in advance meant certain defeat.

But not to ask…to turn her back on all that she knew…

"I'll think about it," she told her parents, hugging each of them and memorizing their faces.

She went to her room and shut the door. The story of Vondiver was in her heart and on her lips and in her mind. It was all that kept the fear at bay. If she gambled and lost, she could still end up destroying Owen. She had to find some way to prevent that from happening. If he even thought that he was responsible for her fate…she was never going to let that happen. If she had to lie a thousand lies, he at least would never suffer from the acts of a headstrong princess.

That night, her mind still awhirl, she left the house. She was nearly to the car when a hand on her arm stopped her.

Delfyne whirled to see Andreus. "I shouldn't have suggested this to you," he said. "I've had time to think now and I realize what a risk it is. I love Owen, but he's hell on women. He might send you away. Your being a princess won't matter a whit to him. Delfyne, think. He might completely break your heart."

Her smile was sad. "Be happy, Dré. Help them to know that I love them and don't want to hurt them."

"Fyna, stop. Now. Really. I'll call them. They'll stop you."

She touched his cheek. "If you try to do that, I'll have to take you down. I can do that, thanks to Owen. And, Dré? I love you. If you ever feel the need to escape, just remember." She put her mouth next to his ear and whispered, "Vondiver." Then she turned.

"Wait! Fyna! What if—what if he won't marry you?"

Pain ripped through her. She was sure that her face blanched.

"I fully expect him to turn me down, Dré," she confided. "The first fifty times I show up, anyway. After that, I'm just hoping that he'll hire me so I can be near him."

Then she ran. She had no doubt that every royal guard in the palace would be right behind her.

Timbelina's tail hit Owen in the eye as he lay under the truck trying to get the damn oil filter off.

"This is no place for a pregnant mother," he told her.

She ignored him as he knew she would and sat down near his head. And the stupid filter still wouldn't come off. He let out a string of curses he almost never used and banged on the thing with the filter wrench.

"Yeah, swearing at it always works." Len's voice came from somewhere east of the truck. "And it isn't going to make Delfyne come back, either."

Owen glowered at the filter, then pulled himself from beneath the truck, washed his hands with the hose and started toward the house. He ignored Len, who was still hanging around.

"Owen, we have to talk. The men sent me."

Okay, now Owen's curiosity was piqued. He turned and saw that the usually laid-back Len had a seriously worried look on his face. "What?" he asked the young vet-to-be.

"We know you love her."

Owen glowered. "I don't." Or at least he would soon be over her. He hoped. Please, let this pain end soon.

"And we know you're in pain," Len went on. "But you're not being careful, and we're worried that you're going to get yourself killed. You nearly got kicked in the head while you were shoeing Doughnut the other day because you weren't paying enough attention. So…we took a vote and we all agree you should take a vacation."

"You took a vote," Owen said.

"Yes."

"And decided I needed a vacation."

"Owen, you were never stupid, so we can tell your heart is torn. Otherwise, you wouldn't be repeating everything I say." Len looked off somewhere to Owen's left as if he couldn't even bear to look at a man so stupid and lovesick. "Now, Delfyne…"

A dull roaring began in Owen's head. "I don't want to talk about Delfyne."

"She was something special, I know."

"I said I don't want to talk about her."

"But the thing is…about Delfyne, I mean…"

Owen didn't know how it happened. He reached out and grabbed Len by the shirt and spun him around. Rage and pain poured through him. "The thing about Delfyne is that she's gone, Len. She's gone." His voice broke.

And Len wasn't even cringing. "The thing about Delfyne," he said, his voice low, "is that I think she may be here. At least, when I looked down the road a few minutes ago there was a cab coming in. I'm pretty sure I saw Delfyne in the backseat."

Owen turned, and there at the end of his drive was a poor excuse of a cab. His heart began to thud erratically like a drummer who had forgotten how to keep time.

He told himself that Len was probably wrong. Delfyne couldn't be here. But then, the door to the car opened and a woman emerged.

For many long seconds Delfyne stared at Owen. Just…stared at him as he stared back. "Why are you treating Len that way?" she finally called.

He let go of Len and the man hit the ground, struggling to regain his footing.

Owen started moving toward Delfyne. "Why are you here?"

"Did you and Len fight? Are you okay?" Concern laced her voice. "What's wrong?"

Ten more steps toward her. "I'm fine. *Len* is fine. He's perfect."

Now she was moving toward him, too. "Owen, I…"

"Why are you here?" he repeated, more forcefully.

And now she seemed to falter. She bit her lip. Delfyne never did things like that. The distance between them couldn't have been more than forty feet but it felt like four hundred. Owen wanted to run to her, grab her up and carry her off.

He fought the urge. He stood as still as he possibly could, but to have given up on ever seeing her again in his life and then to have her here…a firestorm of emotions consumed him. "Delfyne, tell me what's going on," he ordered. "I have to know. Now."

She stood taller and pulled her shoulders back. If ever she had looked the consummate princess, it was in this moment. "For reasons I don't care to go into right now, I'm returning to the States," she said imperiously. "I'm looking for…accommodations, and there isn't much in the area. I'm hoping that you might do me the favor of letting me stay here and possibly work here until I can get settled."

His mind turned to a complete muddle. His heart began to rev like a race car. "Where's the prince?"

She didn't even blink, just kept that gorgeous, stubborn chin high. "I don't know. I don't care."

The joy at having her here paled beside the feeling that something was terribly wrong here. Owen frowned. "Did he hurt you? Did he…damn it, what did he do? He didn't jilt you or…or worse?"

Delfyne shook her head. "He didn't jilt me. He said I couldn't have a cat. He laughed at Timbelina's name." She started walking toward him.

Owen had no idea what she was talking about. All he knew was that she was unharmed and she had seemingly ditched a prince over a cat. "The guy's an idiot. I love that cat," he said.

For the first time she smiled, but it wasn't the totally carefree smile Owen was used to. This one had shades of uncertainty mixed in. It scared him. Petrified him. Someone or something had damaged her.

That did it. He could no longer restrain himself. He started moving toward her, too. Faster. Faster. His long strides ate up the dirt that separated them.

Finally he reached her and he stopped short. They stood there staring at each other.

"Delfyne, I want you to tell me now," he said. "Why are you here?"

"Damn, Owen, didn't you hear her?" Len asked, moving up beside Owen. "The woman wants a place to stay and here you're leaving her dangling and standing in the sun. Don't worry, Delfyne. It's not a problem at all. You can stay at my place."

No. No. No. The words echoed through Owen's mind. As if all the frustration and fear and pain of the past few days and weeks had finally boiled over, Owen whirled and swung at Len. "Like hell she will, cowboy. She's mine."

Len had put up his hands to ward off the blow, and he had barely managed to duck in time, but now he managed a slow smile as he backed away. "Okay, boss. She's yours." Then, he leaned around Owen and peered at Delfyne. "I hope you don't mind too terribly, but I'm retracting my invitation. I need this job…and my unbroken jaw, and it appears you *do* have a place to stay, after all." Then he winked and walked away.

Owen looked at his fist as if he had no idea what it was. He turned back to Delfyne and shook his head. "Forget you heard that. Forget I did that. I'm obviously a complete and total idiot. If you're here, then something monumental and probably scary and terrible has happened. Tell me what it is. Let me help you. For sure, the last thing you need right now is some loose-cannon cowboy like me going all Neanderthal on you and—"

"Owen, stop. Don't apologize. Just…don't. And tell me, did you mean it? Am I really…what you said? Am I yours?"

Delfyne reached out and grabbed his wrists. Her touch was electric, but tough. Maybe even desperate.

Owen looked into her eyes. Tears were streaming down her cheeks. "Oh, love, Delfyne, don't. I'm such a jerk." He cleared the space between them and pulled her into his arms, right up against his heart. "What did I do? Whatever it was, I made it worse, didn't I? Whatever happened, I'll fix it. I'll call someone. I'll make them take you back. I'll call Andreus and make it right. I'll go over there and fight for your rights. They can't kick you out because one prince was a bust. I'll go to battle for you, sweetheart. What do you need me to do?"

"Tell me I'm yours again," she said.

Owen's heart stopped beating completely. A tiny flicker of hope began to ignite, but he fought it. He'd been a madman for days. The fact that he'd nearly decked Len was a sure sign that he was acting crazy. He was unhinged. And if he hoped too hard now, and that hope was crushed again, he might descend into total hell, never to return.

And yet…

"You didn't really mean that, did you?" she asked. "Of course not. You were just…being you. It's that thing you do. You were just trying to protect me from Len because of what had happened in my past."

The flicker became a flame he couldn't battle. "Delfyne, I nearly knocked Len flat, and I'm not the kind of man who hits a friend. My reasons weren't even close to honorable. So, tell me now. Please. Why are you here?"

She stood looking at him with those big sad eyes. His heart just broke. "Please," he said again.

She finally nodded. "All right, I'll tell you. Remember how you told me that this ranch charmed people for the short term but in the long term it might lose its charm?"

"I remember everything."

"Owen, I *love* the ranch," she said, looking up at him defiantly. "I really do. But even if it loses its charm, I'm okay with that. I would have come back even if I hated this place. I just couldn't marry the prince."

He reached out and touched her cheek. "Of course you couldn't. The man didn't understand you."

"Exactly. In fact, you're the only man who's ever really understood me. I had to come tell you that. You made me realize—finally—that being who I really am doesn't mean there's something wrong with me. Even if I'm not a princess anymore. You never made me feel ashamed of being me."

There was something about her voice, about the look in her eyes, about the fact that she had left everything behind and come here in a cab that was practically falling apart. Despite the fact that he was afraid to believe what she seemed to be saying, his fear couldn't matter. At all. He wasn't the important person here now. She was. And she had just said…she'd implied…

"How can a princess just stop being a princess?"

Delfyne stood before him, defiant and beautiful and making his heart hurt just to be near her. "Most princesses can't stop being what they are, I guess, but…I did," she said. "And when I walked away, it was for good. I can't ever change my mind and go back to being a princess again, but that's all right."

Owen studied her. She stood tall and proud, but a tremor of fear still laced her voice. "I suspect there's more to the story," he said.

Her lips trembled. His heart lurched. "There is, of course. Much more, but most of it isn't all that interesting, and anyway, I don't want to talk about that now. Owen, won't you at least kiss me hello, please? I've missed you so much."

All his reservations fell away. He didn't hesitate. He didn't ask more questions. He just scooped her up against his body to cover her mouth with his own. All the desperation of the last few days flooded through him and he couldn't get enough of her. He kissed her three, four, five times.

Get hold of yourself, his brain told him. *She said she wasn't marrying a prince and that she missed you and the ranch. That doesn't necessarily mean that she's staying.* He should ask her a few polite questions, take it slow, get the lay of the land, see if he could be of help to her....

"Stay with me, Delfyne," he whispered against her hair. "I've gone crazy here without you. I'm driving everyone else crazy. I'm even driving the poor cat crazy, I'm so in love with you. How long can you stay?"

"Owen?" Her eyes were big and round and violet and beautiful and...his, he thought again. This tendency to be selfish and possessive had come over him and he couldn't seem to shake it.

"What?" he whispered, as he tried to capture her mouth again.

"You said you loved me."

"I know. I do. I'm mad for you. And yeah, it's probably hopeless. The royal guard is probably on the way to throw me in the dungeon right now."

"That would be very wrong of them when I love you so much, Owen." She kissed his throat, his chin, his mouth. "I came back for you, Owen. Only for you. And I'm not going back to Xenora. I called Andreus, and he's sending all my things so I can stay with you forever."

He kissed her again, then smiled against her mouth. "Then if the guards show up, I'll send them packing. If you want to stay with me, no man had better try to stop you."

"Because I'm yours," she said.

"You've got that right, Princess."

"Forever," she continued.

"At least that long," he agreed. "Marry me?"

"Oh yes," she agreed. "Yes, I demand marriage. In fact, I command you to marry me. Just try to get rid of me this time."

He laughed. "I love it when you go all royal and demanding on me."

"I'll try to remember that," she said with a grin.

"Remember this, too," he said. "You're my home now, my all. Wherever you are, I am. If you want to live somewhere else, I'm there."

"Thank you, Owen, but that's *not* going to happen," she said.

"All right, but if you change your mind, you tell me."

"I won't change my mind." She stood on her toes and wrapped her arms around his neck. "Make me a rancher's wife, Owen."

"I will. And we'll have children if you like. It's time."

She touched his cheek. "You're sure?"

"Never more. I'll always love James. I'll love all our children."

"Then give me children, Owen. Little rancher children."

"Were you always this bossy?" he asked with a grin.

She shrugged. "I used to be a princess."

"And you still are. But now you're my private princess."

"That's the very best kind," Delfyne said, but Owen didn't answer. She was in his arms and all the words that mattered had been spoken.

**We'll be spotlighting a different series
every month throughout 2009
to celebrate our 60th anniversary.**

Look for Harlequin® Historical in May!

Celebrations begin with
a sumptuous Regency house party!

Join three scandalous sisters in

**THE DIAMONDS OF
WELBOURNE MANOR**

Glittering, scintillating, sensual fun
by Diane Gaston, Deb Marlowe
and Amanda McCabe.

**60 years of Harlequin,
600 years of romance
in Harlequin Historical!**

You're invited to join our Tell Harlequin Reader Panel!

By joining our new reader panel you will:

- Receive Harlequin® books—they are FREE and yours to keep with no obligation to purchase anything!
- Participate in fun online surveys
- Exchange opinions and ideas with women just like you
- Have a say in our new book ideas and help us publish the best in women's fiction

In addition, you will have a chance to win great prizes and receive special gifts! See Web site for details. Some conditions apply. Space is limited.

To join, visit us at
www.TellHarlequin.com.

REQUEST YOUR FREE BOOKS!
2 FREE NOVELS PLUS 2
FREE GIFTS!

HARLEQUIN ROMANCE®

From the Heart, For the Heart

YES! Please send me 2 FREE Harlequin Romance® novels and my 2 FREE gifts (gifts are worth about $10). After receiving them, if I don't wish to receive any more books, I can return the shipping statement marked "cancel". If I don't cancel, I will receive 4 brand-new novels every month and be billed just $3.32 per book in the U.S. or $3.80 per book in Canada, plus 25¢ shipping and handling per book and applicable taxes, if any*. That's a savings of over 15% off the cover price! I understand that accepting the 2 free books and gifts places me under no obligation to buy anything. I can always return a shipment and cancel at any time. Even if I never buy another book, the two free books and gifts are mine to keep forever.

114 HDN ERQW   314 HDN ERQ9

Name _____ (PLEASE PRINT)

Address _____ Apt. #

City _____ State/Prov. _____ Zip/Postal Code

Signature (if under 18, a parent or guardian must sign)

Mail to the **Harlequin Reader Service:**
IN U.S.A.: P.O. Box 1867, Buffalo, NY 14240-1867
IN CANADA: P.O. Box 609, Fort Erie, Ontario L2A 5X3

Not valid to current subscribers of Harlequin Romance books.

Want to try two free books from another line?
Call 1-800-873-8635 or visit www.morefreebooks.com.

* Terms and prices subject to change without notice. N.Y. residents add applicable sales tax. Canadian residents will be charged applicable provincial taxes and GST. Offer not valid in Quebec. This offer is limited to one order per household. All orders subject to approval. Credit or debit balances in a customer's account(s) may be offset by any other outstanding balance owed by or to the customer. Please allow 4 to 6 weeks for delivery. Offer available while quantities last.

Your Privacy: Harlequin Books is committed to protecting your privacy. Our Privacy Policy is available online at www.eHarlequin.com or upon request from the Reader Service. From time to time we make our lists of customers available to reputable third parties who may have a product or service of interest to you. If you would prefer we not share your name and address, please check here. ☐

HR08R

Return to Virgin River with a breathtaking
new trilogy from award-winning author

ROBYN CARR

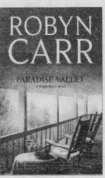

February 2009   March 2009   April 2009

"The Virgin River books are so compelling—
I connected instantly with the characters
and just wanted more and more and more."
—#1 *New York Times* bestselling author
Debbie Macomber

MIRA®

www.MIRABooks.com

MRCTRI09

Coming Next Month

Available May 12, 2009

Next month, Harlequin Romance® brings you
pregnancy and proposals, motherhood and marriage!
And don't forget to make a date with the second book
in our brand-new trilogy, www.blinddatebrides.com!

#4093 ADOPTED: FAMILY IN A MILLION Barbara McMahon
Baby on Board
Searching for his adopted son, Zack discovers sexy single mom Susan.
But she has no idea how inextricably their paths are linked....

#4094 HIRED: NANNY BRIDE Cara Colter
Baby on Board
On meeting playboy tycoon Joshua, nanny Dannie begins to see that
there is more to the man than designer suits. She wishes he could see
the real her, too.

#4095 ITALIAN TYCOON, SECRET SON Lucy Gordon
Baby on Board
Disaster brought Mandy love when she was stranded in an avalanche
with gorgeous Italian Renzo. But a year later, will he still want to claim
her—and their son?

#4096 BLIND-DATE BABY Fiona Harper
www.blinddatebrides.com
After finding love with handsome stranger Noah when her daughter
signs her up for an Internet-dating site, it's time for flirty forty-year-old
Grace to embrace motherhood once again!

#4097 THE BILLIONAIRE'S BABY Nicola Marsh
Baby on Board
Billionaire Blane wants the only thing money can't buy—to win back his
wife, Cam. As he romances her under the sizzling Australian sun, will
their spark reignite?

#4098 DOORSTEP DADDY Shirley Jump
Baby on Board
Writer Dalton demands solitude, not a baby on his doorstep! But when
single mom Ellie and her baby come into his life, it's time for Dalton to
start a whole new chapter....

HRCNMBPA0409